Easing back a tempting inch, she regarded him through her lashes. "I can feel the conflict in you, Eli. I know what it's like to want but know you can't or shouldn't have. I think."

"That's part of our problem, isn't it?" His eyes traveled over her face. "We're always thinking."

Her smile widened. "Not sure I'd say that, Lieutenant."

And yanking his mouth back down onto hers blasted everything that didn't have its roots in need from his head.

It might have been lightning or the glow from the taper that caused the darkness to shift.

Whatever the source, when he spotted a shadow that shouldn't be there, his body stilled....

RAVEN'S HOLLOW

JENNA RYAN

Recycling programs
for this product may
not exist in your area.

To my dad, Bill Goff.

It's been a long road, and there's more to go.

Please, don't forget....

ISBN-13: 978-0-373-69745-8

RAVEN'S HOLLOW

Copyright © 2014 by Jacqueline Goff

All rights reserved. Except for use in any review, the reproduction or
utilization of this work in whole or in part in any form by any electronic,
mechanical or other means, now known or hereafter invented, including
xerography, photocopying and recording, or in any information storage
or retrieval system, is forbidden without the written permission of the
publisher, Harlequin Enterprises Limited, 225 Duncan Mill Road,
Don Mills, Ontario M3B 3K9, Canada.

This is a work of fiction. Names, characters, places and incidents are
either the product of the author's imagination or are used fictitiously,
and any resemblance to actual persons, living or dead, business
establishments, events or locales is entirely coincidental.

This edition published by arrangement with Harlequin Books S.A.

For questions and comments about the quality of this book,
please contact us at CustomerService@Harlequin.com.

® and TM are trademarks of Harlequin Enterprises Limited or its
corporate affiliates. Trademarks indicated with ® are registered in the
United States Patent and Trademark Office, the Canadian Trade Marks
Office and in other countries.

Printed in U.S.A.

www.Harlequin.com

ABOUT THE AUTHOR

Jenna started making up stories before she could read or write. As she grew up, romance always had a strong appeal, but romantic suspense was the perfect fit. She tried out a number of different careers, including modeling, interior design and travel, but her one true love has always been writing. That and her longtime partner, Rod.

Inspired from book to book by her sister Kathy, she lives in a rural setting fifteen minutes from the city of Victoria, British Columbia. It's taken a lot of years, but she's finally slowed the frantic pace and adopted a West Coast mindset. Stay active, stay healthy, keep it simple. Enjoy the ride, enjoy the read. All of that works for her, but what she continues to enjoy most is writing stories she loves. She also loves reader feedback. Email her at jacquigoff@shaw.ca or visit Jenna Ryan on Facebook.

Books by Jenna Ryan

CAST OF CHARACTERS

Sadie Bellam—She owns the local newspaper—and the person who killed her cousin twenty years ago wants her dead.

Eli Blume—This New York cop has sworn to unmask Sadie's monstrous stalker.

Tyler Blume—The Hollow's police chief was angry when Sadie ended their engagement.

Brady Blume—Does the local veterinarian know where the monster lives?

Orley Bellam—Sadie's cousin hates being the descendant of a witch.

Molly Bellam—She has the witchy blood of her ancestor, and the personality to match.

Laura Bellam-Blume—Eli's stepsister was murdered two decades ago in Raven's Bog.

Cal Kilgore—Everyone thought Laura's ex killed her, yet he remains free.

Chapter One

She was being hunted.

The darkness seethed with the bloodlust of the fanatics behind her. She couldn't see them, couldn't see anything except the shadows of the hollow that twisted branches into skeletal limbs and turned everything that moved into her persecutors. The shadows hid their faces, and their bodies, but the footsteps shaking the forest floor told her they were closing in.

An ancient name swam in Sadie's head even as desperation drove her deeper into the woods. Nola Bellam. Not her, not quite, but someone who was part of her.

The knowledge did nothing to alter her flight. Fear gathered like a fiery liquid in her chest, blocking logic, preventing clear thought. The trees, misshapen and grown together, bent lower. The ground grew rougher, the bushes more tangled. Wind swooped down in bursts to claw at her black robe.

She'd run from these same pursuers many times before tonight, as herself and as her ancestor. She was fast, but they were faster, and one of them was equally desperate.

Ezekiel Blume had raped Nola Bellam, who'd been his brother's wife. Nola had taken her child and escaped, but not to safety. Nowhere was safe in Raven's Hollow. Ezekiel had been hell-bent on capturing her before his brother returned to the area. On killing her before the truth came out.

Because ignorance was the mightiest weapon of all, he'd branded her a witch and set a group of fearful townspeople on her. He'd died for that in the end. They all had. His brother, Hezekiah, had ensured it.

Words and images blurred. Ravens dived now with the wind. One of them, as large as a man, landed on the path several yards ahead.

Something about him penetrated the haze in Sadie's mind, and she slowed.

"Keep running," he ordered, but she wouldn't. It was time to make things right.

Moonbeams silvered the trees. Ezekiel's knife slashed the air while his mob of followers held their torches high, circled and salivated.

Smiling at their fervor, Sadie raised her arms and let the glittering darkness enfold her.

When Ezekiel's blade struck, pain shot through every nerve in her body. A single cry kept the man-sized raven away. Tonight, the war was hers to wage.

So let it hurt. Let her blood be spilled. This time she wouldn't try to trick death. She would accept her fate, and in doing so, she would save a man from the evil that stalked him here in the heart of the hollow.

As she lowered her arms, a knife slid from her sleeve into her palm. Resolved, she closed her fingers around it. She saw Ezekiel's face in the gloom, lit from within by the madness that consumed him.

When his blade fell yet again, she aimed and plunged her own into his chest.

His eyes widened, his hand stilled. His body froze beneath its cloak.

Ezekiel dropped to the ground at her feet, blood flowing like a river from his wound.

Sadie's breath rushed out. She'd stopped him. There was no longer a reason for the evil to be called up, no need for the poison within it to destroy an innocent soul. The man-sized raven would turn back into what he had been, what he still should be, and life would resume its normal rhythm.

Yet when she turned to watch the separation occur, her heart stuttered.

The raven stood, as solid and malevolent as ever, half bird, half man, staring at her through eyes that glowed red and vengeful.

"What is done cannot be undone, Sadie Bellam. You have your own battle to fight, and he who is me to help you conquer what comes."

What did he mean, he who was him? Frustration linked with fear even as the creature closed enormous black wings around his body and dissolved into the night.

It started slowly, a mere thread of sound beneath the raging wind. She spun back, but saw nothing. No one.

"Daughter of the witch." Laughter permeated the silky voice slithering into her head. "Do not be deceived. There is no one in the hollow who can help you. All that you see tonight, your mind has conjured…except for me!"

The voice rose to a roar as another cloaked shape reared up. This one wielded a much larger knife than Ezekiel's. She saw a gleam of insanity in the eyes that locked briefly on hers.

"Your blade struck a false mark, Sadie Bellam. Be assured, mine will not!"

As the knife pierced her skin, pain exploded in Sadie's chest. She knew then what it was to die. The taste of it was bitter copper in her throat.

The hollow faded in and out, and her mind spiraled into

a pool of black. An iron fist closed around her lungs. She saw claws reaching for her from above.

And woke as she always did—gasping for air on the floor beside her bed.

Chapter Two

"Variations on a theme."

Standing on the sidewalk outside the pharmacy in Raven's Hollow, Maine, Sadie rubbed the lingering chill from her bare arms and willed the nightmare that had spawned it away.

But the ice in her veins wasn't something her mind, or the unseasonal warm spell that had the early October temperatures hovering in the low eighties, could affect. It was simply there, so often in recent days that she was growing inured to it.

"You could exercise before you go to sleep," her cousin Molly suggested.

"Tried it. Didn't help."

"You said the dreams vary. In what way?"

Sadie considered for a moment. "The cast of characters is always the same. It's the setting that changes. But no matter where it plays out, I wind up on my bedroom floor, gasping for air and checking for blood."

"It sounds—not like fun. Especially the checking-for-blood part. Do you think you could be possessed? Or maybe channeling our ancestor?"

"You think I'm channeling a three-hundred-year-old ghost?" Even knowing Molly was serious, Sadie quirked her lips. "Okay, I doubt that. And possession's even more out there. My guess is it's a residual memory."

"Of our cousin Laura's death?"

Dropping both her sunglasses and a firm mental shield in place, Sadie regarded the cloudless blue sky over Raven's Hollow. "The anniversary of her murder's coming up in ten days."

"Yes, but, Sadie, Laura died twenty years ago."

"I know. Look, this topic's too uncomfortable for me right now. I need to move past it before I spook myself into doing something ridiculous, like consulting a hypnotist. All I wanted when I came into the drugstore was to show you a preview of tomorrow's B-Section headline." At Molly's level stare, she rolled her eyes. "Yes, fine, and buy a bottle of Tylenol."

Satisfied, her cousin lifted the ponytail from her neck. "You've bought two bottles of Tylenol in the last week, Sadie. You don't usually go through that many in a whole year." She frowned. "Meaning you have a problem either at home or at the newspaper. And since you put in three years with the *Philadelphia Inquirer* and two more with the *Washington Post,* I can't see our Mini-Me daily overstressing you. So, home it is. And seeing as you live alone…"

"Right, good, got it." Sadie waved her to a halt. "Your deductive skills are as sharp as ever—and FYI, the offer for you to come and help me run the *Chronicle* stands."

Her cousin's mouth compressed. "You know I'm not good with people."

"Molly, you're a pharmacist. You talk to people all day long."

"I'm in control—well, sort of in control behind the counter. Reporters have to wade into unfamiliar territory and be cheerful, sneaky, sly, whatever it takes to gain an interviewee's confidence."

"I said help me run the paper, not trick your friends and neighbors into telling you all their dirty little secrets."

Molly let her ponytail drop and her shoulders hunch. "I hear plenty of secrets without wading or tricking. Too many some days. Example, Ben Leamer's sister came in this morning."

"Ah." Sadie worked up a smile. "Boils or hemorrhoids?"

"Both. She went into detail for forty minutes."

"And I'm complaining about a few nightmares. Having said that, and seriously hoping you won't elaborate on the state of Dorothy Leamer's hemorrhoids, I'll ask again, what did you think of my headline?" She dangled the sample copy for her cousin to see.

Raven's Cove's Oldest Resident Breezes Into His Second Century.

"It's good." Molly pushed her hands into the pockets of her smock. "The photo of old Rooney in his cottage is perfect."

"Why do I sense a but?"

"Don't you think you're rushing things a bit? Rooney Blume's birthday is two weeks away."

"And the *Chronicle* will be running stories about his extremely colorful life until he reaches that landmark date."

"That's the point. What if he doesn't?"

"Reach the landmark? Why wouldn't he?"

"Because he's a hundred years old. He could die any day. Any minute. Writing ahead might jinx him."

Tipping her sunglasses down, Sadie stared. "Have you met the man? Rhetorical question," she said before her cousin could respond. "He smoked a pipe until he was ninety-two. I hate to think how much whiskey he knocks back in a day. He tells dirty jokes nonstop at the dockside bar that's basically his second home in the Cove, then laughs until his face turns bright red. If none of those things have gotten him, me writing a series of articles two weeks ahead isn't likely to do it."

Molly's chin came up in a rare show of defiance. "Maybe that's what your recurring dreams mean."

"What, you think they're telling me not to fly in the face of God and/or fate? They're stories, Molly. Feel-good articles that will, I hope, help stop the residents of our twin towns from going for each other's throats every time one's name is mentioned to the other. I'm sure this kind of resent-the-twin thing doesn't happen in Minneapolis or St. Paul."

"Raven's Hollow and Raven's Cove aren't twin towns. We're more like evil stepsisters. The Cove has nasty raven legends. We have a history of witches. You'll never mesh those two things. Just—never."

As if cued, a man Sadie recognized from Raven's Cove strolled past. His name was Samuel Blume. He carried a racing form and a rabbit's foot in one hand and a copy of the *Chronicle* in the other. A huge smile split his weathered face.

"Afternoon, ladies. I see you're forecasting big rain and wind tonight, Sadie. Must be your Bellam blood rearing its witchy head, because the radio and TV both say sunny and hot for at least three more days."

She shrugged. "You choose, Sam. My newspaper's going with the rain and wind."

"Good thing I brought my lucky charm. I'll be sure to get myself out of here and home safe before whatever storm you're brewing up hits."

"I rest my case," Molly said when the man moved along. "We're Bellams, he's a Blume. He assumes we're all like our ancestor. It's a battle of sarcastic wills. Hollow witches versus Cove ravens. Whose legends pack a bigger wallop?"

"Well, now you're getting weird." Sadie used the folded preview edition of the *Chronicle* to fan her face. "We're not supernatural versions of the Hatfields and McCoys, and we're definitely not Cinderella's stepsisters in town form. Besides, the Raven's Hollow police chief's a Blume, and he doesn't believe in legends at all. So pax, and thanks for the Tylenol."

Sadie turned to leave, but a tiny sound from Molly stopped her.

"Problem?" she asked, turning back.

"No. It's just—you look very nice today."

Sadie glanced down at her green-black tank top, her long, floaty skirt and high wedge sandals. "Thank you—I think."

"You seem more city than town to me."

"Okay." Her eyebrows went up. "Does that mean something?"

"I wonder how long you'll stay."

"I've been here for two years so far, plus the seven I put in as a kid."

"I've been here my whole life. You have a transient soul, Sadie. I think you'll eventually get bored with the Hollow and move on."

"Maybe." She waited a beat before asking, "Is that a bad thing?"

"For you, no. But others belong here."

It took Sadie a moment to figure out where this was going. Then she followed her cousin's gaze to the police station and heard the click.

"Ty and I were only engaged for a few months. We realized our mistake, ended the engagement and now we're friends." Her eyes sparkled. "A Bellam and a Blume, Molly. Can you imagine the repercussions if we'd challenged the natural order of things and followed through with a wedding? Although," she added, "it's been done before, and neither the Hollow nor the Cove fell into the Atlantic as a result."

"Are you teasing me?"

"Yes, and I'm sorry. Really. I know you like Ty. It's good. I like him, too, just not the way a potential life mate should."

Molly's cheeks went pink. "Everyone likes Ty. I didn't mean—I don't have a thing for him."

"No? Weird," Sadie repeated. She grinned. "Bye, Molly."

"Bye, Sadie."

With a quick—and she had to admit—somewhat guilty glance at the station house, Sadie started off again.

The fact that it took her fifteen minutes to make what should have been a two-minute walk no longer surprised her. Ten people stopped her on the sidewalk to jab fingers at the clear blue sky. Thankfully, only three of the ten inquired about the source of the *Chronicle*'s forecast.

She didn't think any of those three actually believed in witches of the warts-and-pointed-hats variety, but more than a few of them probably subscribed to the notion that Hezekiah Blume, founder and first citizen of nearby Raven's Cove, had, upon marrying Nola Bellam, in reality wed a witch.

According to Cove legend, the union had led to a fatal fallout between Hezekiah and his younger brother, Ezekiel. Ezekiel had tried to kill Nola, Hezekiah had ultimately killed Ezekiel, and the entire tragedy had ended with the gates of hell blasting open between the two towns—in the literal sense back then and still in a figurative one today.

Taking her right back, Sadie thought with a sigh, to the beginning of last night's dream.

Resisting an urge to swallow more pills, she pushed through the doors of the wood and stone building that housed the *Chronicle*.

She'd inherited the newspaper from her uncle two years ago. Next to the techno-sleek environs she'd known in Boston and D.C., it was a New England dinosaur, complete with antique wiring, fifty-year-old basement presses and fourteen employees for whom the word *change* had little or no meaning.

It had taken her the better part of a year to nudge the place past the millennium mark in terms of equipment. The employees continued to be a work in progress. But she considered it a major step forward that several of them had gone from calling her Ms. Bellam to Sadie over the past year.

She spent the remainder of the afternoon reviewing advertising layouts with her copy editor. At seven o'clock precisely, the man creaked to his feet. "My knees have been acting up all day, Sadie. Figure you could be right about that storm after all."

"The weather center in Bangor could be right," she countered. "I'm only the messenger."

"Said Tituba to her inquisitor." With a wink and a grin, he limped off down the hall.

"I give up." Rising from her desk, Sadie rocked her head from side to side. "Call me a witch. Call everyone with the same last name as me a witch. Make the nightmares I've been having go away, and I'll accept pretty much any label at this point."

She knew she'd be putting in at least another hour before packing up her laptop and heading home. With luck, a little overtime would help her sleep better. Unless the predicted storm arrived with thunder and wound up sparking another dream.

"Well, Jesus, Sadie," she laughed, and forced herself to buckle down.

She had the ad layouts sorted, two columns edited and

was endeavoring to make sense of a third when the phone rang.

With her mind still on the article—who used Tabasco sauce as an emergency replacement for molasses in oatmeal cookies?—she picked up.

"Raven's Hollow *Chronicle,* Sadie Bellam speaking."

For a moment there was nothing, then a mechanical whisper reached her. "Look at your computer, Sadie."

The darkest aspects of the nightmare rushed back in to ice her skin. Her fingers tightened on the handset. "Who is this?"

"Look at your in-box. See the card I've sent you."

Her eyes slid to the monitor. She wanted to brush it off as a bad joke. Wanted to, but couldn't. Using a breathing technique to bolster her courage, she complied.

"Do you see it?"

Her heart tripped as the image formed. The "card" showed two animated ravens. One was locked inside a cage. The other was out. The free bird used a talon to scratch a word in what looked to be blood. It said simply:

MINE!

Chapter Three

"You about done changing that tire, Elijah?" Despite the pouring rain, Rooney Blume stuck his head out the window of his great-grandson's truck. He squinted skyward as thunder rattled the ground. "Someone upstairs must be working off one big mad."

"Someone out here definitely is," Eli said, giving the lug nuts he'd just put on the tire a hard cinch to tighten them. "What were you thinking riding your bike to the Cove in this weather?"

"DMV lifted my license last year, and the sun was shining when I started out. Probably good you came along when you did, though. My balance tends to fail me in the wet."

As Eli recalled, his great-grandfather's balance wasn't a whole lot better in the dry. There'd also been a thermos of heavily spiked tea tucked in the bike's carrier, and likely close to half of what he'd started out with inside the old man by the time their paths had crossed.

Right now Rooney was pushing a metal cup through the window. Giving the last nut a tug, Eli accepted the cup, considered briefly, then tossed the contents back in a single fiery shot.

Some things, he realized, when the flames in his throat subsided, never changed. He gave the cup back to Rooney.

His great-grandfather pointed a knobby finger at a line of trees bent low by the wind. "Gonna be a bitch of a night."

Soaked to the skin, with his dark hair dripping in his eyes and rainwater running down his neck, Eli climbed back inside and started the truck's engine. "You think?" But he grinned as he spoke, and flicked a hand at the thermos. "I'm surprised that tea of yours hasn't eaten through the aluminum casing by now."

"You sound like my great-grandson."

"I am your great-grandson."

"I mean the other one. The one who's wearing a police chief's badge and sporting a big dose of attitude over in the Hollow."

"Only a town of fools would give a badge to someone who prefers carrot juice to whiskey." Eli squinted through the streaming windshield. "Self-denial that unswerving upsets the balance of the universe."

"Spoken like a cop after my own heart. And while we're on the subject of badges and balances, did you know your carrot-loving cousin's not gonna be putting a wedding ring on Sadie Bellam's finger?"

"Heard about it." Eli kept his tone casual and swept his gaze across the mud-slick road. "I also heard it was Sadie who ended the engagement."

Rooney's expression grew canny. "You got awful good hearing for a man who spends most of his time hunting down killers in New York City."

"It's not so far from there to here. As the raven flies."

The old man chortled and offered him another cup of "tea." "I won't say you're a jackass, Elijah, only that among other more valuable things—and for 'things,' read 'Sadie'—the badge on Ty's chest could've been yours if you'd wanted it."

"And an executive position at the *New York Times* could've been Sadie's if she'd wanted it. We do what we do, Rooney, and live with the consequences."

His great-grandfather made a rude sound. "You're as stubborn as twenty mules, the pair of you. You knew each other as kids, connection was already there. Life'll take you down different paths because that's how it goes sometimes. But it goes in circles other times, and you and Sadie came to the end of a doozy when you met up last April in Boston."

"Rooney—" Eli began.

"I was there, Eli. I saw you. And let me tell you, there wasn't a soul at that wedding reception who even noticed the bride and groom with the fireworks you two set off. Suddenly, next thing I know, Sadie's back at the *Chronicle*, and you're tracking a serial killer through the underbelly of Manhattan. Me, the universe and pretty much everyone at the reception are still scratching our heads over *that* turn of events."

Eli sighed. "You, the universe and pretty much everyone at the reception read too much into a time-and-place chemical reaction. Sadie was engaged in April."

"Only until she got back from Boston. Two days later, your cousin Ty was drowning his sorrows in goat milk and a double dose of wheat germ."

"Sadie's not ready to be married, and my life's good the way it is. Cops and relationships don't mix."

Rooney snorted. "If you expect me to buy that load of bull, you're no kind of cop. And no kin of mine."

"In that case, happy hundred and first in advance, and I'll be heading back to New York right after I drop you off at Joe's bar."

"I need a favor before you go."

"Yeah?" Eli raised a mildly amused brow. "I could

say I don't do favors for people who claim to have dis-owned me."

"But that would make you unworthy of any badge, and we both know that's as far from the truth as it gets."

The vague humor lingered despite the fact that Eli could no longer see either the road or the dense woods next to it that stretched from the Cove to the Hollow and beyond. The rain fell in blinding sheets now. "What do you need?"

"Ty's on duty tonight. I want you to go by his office in the Hollow. He's got a bulldog there named Chopper. Family in town's heading south and can't take him, so I said I'd think about it."

"You want a dog?"

"Don't give me that look, Eli. If I die before Chopper does, I'll leave him to you."

"Still a cop here. I can't have pets."

"No pets, no women. You're not a cop, you're a monk."

"Who said anything about no women?"

"No women of consequence, then. Now, you take my last serious relationship versus the last woman I had sex with."

"Jesus, Rooney."

The old man drank from his thermos before offering back a mostly toothless smile. "You think because I'm old I don't have sex?"

"Yes—no. Dammit, I don't think about it one way or the other." Ever.

"Why not? I'm human."

"You're also my great-grandfather, and I do my level best to keep thoughts of sex, parents and grandparents out of my head."

"You're a prude, Elijah. Doesn't bother me to picture you with a woman."

The first bolt of lightning shot down deep in the hollow. "Are we actually having this conversation?"

"I am." Rooney peered into his thermos. "Seems to me you're doing more avoiding than conversing."

Eli swerved around a barely visible pothole. "What I'm doing is trying to figure out how anybody's sex life, mine included, relates to me checking out a bulldog."

"So you'll do it?"

"What, have sex or check out the dog?"

"In a perfect world, both, but I'll settle for the dog and enjoy thinking about you and Ty firing daggers at each other while you picture, but deliberately don't talk about, the lovely Sadie Bellam."

"You have a wide streak of mean in you, old man." But a slow grin removed the sting of Eli's remark. In any case, glaring down his resentful cousin would be hell-and-gone preferable to visualizing Rooney naked with a woman.

As the wind picked up, and the truck began to buck, even his garrulous great-grandfather stopped talking. The road, such as it was, became a river, complete with currents, broken branches and sinkholes that could rip out the undercarriage should Eli happen to hit one. That he didn't was more of a miracle in his opinion than a testament to his driving skills.

Twenty minutes later, he pulled up outside his second cousin's shabby dockside bar, Two Toes Joe's. He saw Rooney safely through the door, turned down a mug of coppery green beer—old Joe really should have his lines changed—and jogged back to his still-running truck.

The dashboard clock read 9:30, which surprised him since it seemed to have been dark for hours. If he'd believed in omens, as at least three-quarters of his relatives in the area did, he'd check out the dog—couldn't not do that—then say screw an early arrival for Rooney's birthday and return to New York. Return to sanity, and more important, the safety of a no-Sadie zone.

What had flared between them last April had been unexpected and intense. Sadie had been a kid the last time he'd seen her. Seven years old and shocked speechless over the murder of her cousin Laura, who'd also happened to be his stepsister.

Although the residents of both Raven's Cove and Raven's Hollow had been horrified, few had been as badly shaken as he and Sadie. How could anyone who'd never had the misfortune to do so possibly understand what it felt like to discover the body of someone you loved? And not merely discover, but, in Sadie's case, literally stumble over.

Her family had left Raven's Hollow six months later. His had stuck it out for another six years, searching for a closure they'd never received.

To this day, Laura's killer remained at large. A handful of suspects and numerous persons of interest had been questioned and released. Over time—two decades at this point—what had started as a countywide manhunt had been reduced to a dusty homicide report in the back of the sheriff's filing cabinet. Clues gathered at the scene had resulted in nothing, and, as they so often did in situations like these, the case had gone cold.

For Eli, the memory of Laura's murder had dimmed but never disappeared. Not completely. Every similar crime he worked to solve these days took him back to her death. When that happened, the raw pain and guilt would slam through him as hard as it had done the evening he and Sadie had met in the hollow.

On a less grisly note, Eli couldn't deny that, even at seven years of age, Sadie Bellam had been a beauty. Fast-forward twenty years, slide her into a clingy silver dress, and she'd quite literally stripped the breath from his lungs.

He'd prowled around the edges of that Boston reception hall, watching but not approaching her for thirty wary minutes, until one of her aunts had swept in and sealed the deal by insisting they dance.

The idea of taking the memory deeper tempted, but unfortunately, a gust of wind upward of forty miles an hour had other ideas. It grabbed his four-by-four and sent it sliding toward a deep gully. Eli rode the wave, felt the kick of wind abate and urged the truck back onto the road.

It had been a sunny seventy-eight degrees when he'd left New York City. The clear skies had held to Bangor. Then, less than ten miles from the Cove, a mass of boiling black clouds had rolled in and let go.

He glanced left as thunder rumbled up and out of the hollow. Jagged forks of lightning split the sky overhead. His truck, three years old and heavy as hell, shuddered through another blast of wind.

Only a seriously disturbed person would stay out in this. Would *be* out in this. The dog could have waited while he went head-to-head with a glass of Joe's toxic beer.

Without warning, twin beams of light appeared directly ahead. They slashed through the murk, momentarily blinding him. Swearing, Eli jerked the steering wheel hard, felt the truck's back end fishtail and had to compensate to keep the entire vehicle from tumbling into the ravine.

He might have won the battle if something—tree, car or possibly both—hadn't become a sudden and solid roadblock in front of him.

Using his forward momentum, together with muscle and brakes, he went for a one-eighty turn. But the mass was too close and the road too slick for him to gain the traction necessary to execute it.

The collision sent his head and shoulder into the side window. A clap of thunder underscored the hit, but the sound was nothing more than a murmur in Eli's mind. By the time the truck stopped moving, the storm, the night and the hollow had faded to black around him.

Chapter Four

"Eli, can you hear me?"

A woman's voice reached him. Possibly Sadie's, possibly not. She was far away but definitely calling his name. Did that mean he was alive? Because if not, he'd gone someplace dark, wet and incredibly uncomfortable.

"Eli, damn it, open the door!"

Someplace where the angels—at worst, he hoped, angels—shouted orders, and every thought was coated in a bloodred haze.

The haze pulsed for several seconds before subsiding to a repetitive and annoying thud.

He cracked his eyes open to a different kind of darkness. This one was loud and it moved. Both sound and motion jabbed at him like dull knives. He was tempted to sink back under until it stopped.

"Wake up, Eli, and open the door."

Sadie's voice—he was sure of it now—sounded impatient, yet held the barest hint of a tremor. He let the memory of her face draw him to the surface and most of the way through it to consciousness.

Levering himself upright, he swore. And kept swearing because it helped him clear out the last of the haze. Once it was gone, he located and hit the lock release.

The door shot open. It very nearly flew off its hinges

judging from the screech of metal and the ferocious howl of the wind that grabbed it. Eli managed to clamp a hand on to Sadie's arm before the unexpected backward motion sent her into the ravine.

He'd forgotten she had the balance of a mountain goat. Without missing a beat, she bunched his wet T-shirt and gave him a hard shake. "Are you hurt?"

He almost smiled. "Been better. Need a minute for my brain to settle."

"In that case, Lieutenant, shift your excellent butt to the passenger side, and let me in."

Not quite a storybook angel, but close enough. He grinned. "Helluva time to decide you want to do what we managed not to do in Boston."

With a glance into the hollow, she pushed on his shoulder. "If we do now what we didn't do, this really thin rock ledge that your rear tires are barely sitting on is going to crumble apart and send us straight to hell. Or into Raven's Bog. Jury's still out on which name's more appropriate."

Either place was jarring enough for him to snap his head around.

"Bet that hurt—" she began, then gasped when he lifted her inside and deposited her on the passenger seat. "What are you doing?"

"Don't move." He reached for the ignition key.

Swinging her legs around and down, she snagged his wrist. "The engine's running, Eli. You just can't hear it over the Tarzan roar of testosterone in your brain."

"Pretty sure I spun out trying to avoid a head-on with your vehicle, Sadie."

Keeping an eye on the rearview mirror, and using a spectacular bolt of lightning to aid his vision, Eli shoved the truck in gear. After several seconds of maneuvering, he crawled it away from the edge.

Sadie let out a relieved breath. "I'd be impressed if I didn't know for a fact that I could have done the same thing a full minute sooner."

"We're not on a deadline, sweetheart." He fingered a cut on his forehead, and wasn't surprised when he spied a smear of blood. "Are you hurt, and did we hit?"

"No, I'm not, and yes, we did. But not each other." In the process of wringing out her long red-brown hair, she nodded at the windshield. "It's difficult to see right now, but that big black thing in front of us is a pine tree. It started to fall, I hit the brakes. At the risk of fueling your already massive ego, you must have done one wicked spinout to avoid being flattened by something that could have pancaked an eighteen-wheeler."

"Speaking of." Eli sized up the tilt of his truck's back end. "Unless one of my tires is sitting in a hole, I've got a flat."

She waved a hand in front of his face. "Did I mention the tree was huge, with the potential to destroy both you and your vehicle?" A frustrated sound emerged. "Why are you even on this road, Eli? Why are you in Maine at all for that matter?"

"Did you think I wouldn't come for Rooney's hundred and first?"

"No, I figured you'd come, just not until the last minute."

"I'd be offended if I wasn't sure about that flat and apparently in need of a lift."

She stabbed at the windshield, repeated very clearly, "Big tree, tremendous crushing power."

His lips curved. "Yeah, I get the luck part. What I haven't got is a second spare."

He told her, in bullet points, about Rooney, the bicycle that was currently strapped to his roof rack and Joe's bar.

Laughing, she dropped her head back onto the seat. "If I said any of that surprised me, I'd be lying." She slanted him a speculative look. "Still a little shocked to see you, though. On this road. At this time of night."

"Right back at you. And don't tell me you didn't know there was a storm rolling in."

"I knew," she agreed, far too softly for his liking.

He studied her profile in the next flash of lightning. "Something's wrong."

"Nothing I can't handle."

With his brain back on track, he reached out and wrapped his fingers around her neck. "You were driving from the Hollow to the Cove, Sadie, in weather no sane person would take on without extremely strong incentive. As I recall, you're stubborn, but relatively sane."

She started to speak, then broke off and grabbed his chin as lightning snaked through the clouds. "You're bleeding!"

"A little. It's not…" He hissed when she poked at the gash. "Well, it *was* going numb."

"Sorry." She lightened her touch and her tone. "Eli, you were barely conscious when I found you. You could have a concussion."

"I could also be halfway back to New York. Might have been except for a damn bulldog. Don't ask. Just trust me when I tell you I've been hit on the head more times than I can count."

She formed her lips into a smile. "To which I'll simply say, no comment—and you can let go of me now."

"I will, just as soon as you tell me why you were heading to the Cove in a storm that scared Rooney spitless for close to twenty minutes."

"I—seriously?"

"Talk to me, Sadie."

She blew out a breath. "Fine, I got an email. It was—unusual. I don't know how or why, but it also seemed familiar. Like a memory buried deep in my head. So deep I can't visualize it."

"You got a familiar feeling from an email?"

"Well, I say feeling. It was more like a punch of pure creepy. And a strong sense that the sender was watching me."

"Was he?"

"I don't see how. I was in my office at the *Chronicle*. The guy on the phone couldn't have..." She halted there, bit her lip. "I, uh, didn't mention him, did I?"

"Not unless my brain's shorting, and I doubt that." Because his fingers were still curled around her neck, she couldn't draw away. That she made no effort to do so told him a great deal—most of it not good. She was scared. "What did the guy on the phone want?"

"If I knew that, I wouldn't have been going to the Cove in a storm that scared your great-grandfather spitless." Her eyes, as gray and stormy as the night, slid past him to the trails of mud that slithered down the driver's window. "The ravens must be significant."

Eli's grip tightened. "You wanna back that up for me?"

"The card was animated. One of the ravens was inside a cage, the other was out. The outside one scratched the word MINE in blood with his talon. I freaked at first, but after a while I convinced myself it was no big deal."

"How long's a while?"

"Not sure, maybe fifteen minutes. Afterward, I decided to proofread a column I'd imported for the weekend edition about fanatics and the rising numbers of them who've begun to act on their so-called beliefs. And there I was, right back to freaked. Seeing as he knows everything raven-related, I figured the best thing to do would be talk to Rooney, who, in case you're unaware, never answers his phone."

"I am aware of that, actually." But Eli's response was preoccupied as he searched his mind for—something. "A raven in a cage," he repeated. "Why can I almost picture that?"

"No idea, but please tell me there isn't a legend in the Cove about this kind of thing."

"Not that I know of, and it's the card part that's ringing a really distant bell."

"That bell could be your head still ringing from the whack it took when you almost wound up in the bog."

"There is that," he agreed.

When thunder caused the ground to tremble, she stared straight into his eyes. "You know where we are, don't you."

It wasn't a question, Eli reflected. "Yeah, I know. This is where you and I met the night we discovered Laura's body."

"Met, argued, walked and found."

"It's been two decades, Sadie."

"I have a long, and vivid, memory."

"Ditto, but right now I have a more immediate problem."

The breath she released ended on a laugh. "You really don't, you know. You've got a flat and no spare, which means your vehicle's stranded. Mine, on the other hand, has all four tires intact. Seeing as it's on the other side of the pine, the Hollow as a destination wins by default." A light danced up into her eyes. "Looks like you get to check out that bulldog after all, Lieutenant."

"Yeah, well." He moved too quickly for her to react. One moment, his gaze was sliding across her mouth. The next, his own was covering it.

The last thought Eli had before his brain shut down was that kissing Sadie Bellam would be either the best thing he'd ever do or the worst mistake he'd ever make.

Chapter Five

For a suspended moment, Sadie's mind and senses blanked. Then everything inside began to sizzle and snap.

She hadn't kissed him in Boston. Oh, she'd wanted to, too many times to count, but whenever she'd thought about it, the ring on her finger had become a lead weight reminding her that she was engaged to another man.

There was no ring on her finger now, Sadie's overheated senses pointed out. But that still didn't make kissing him a good idea.

Unfortunately, the sound that emerged from her throat more closely resembled a purr than a protest. She also suspected the fingers she'd curled into his hair were holding his mouth on hers rather than trying to push him away.

Fascination wove a greedy path through the sparks. Eli was seducing her with his lips and tongue, with his whole mouth, in fact. Although it was difficult to form a thought, Sadie wondered if she'd ever been kissed quite this thoroughly before. If she had—and she doubted it—the memory eluded her.

A crackle of lightning preceded another ground-shaking peal of thunder. The storm sounds matched the heat currently shooting through her veins. With her fisted hands, she tugged him closer. She wanted to climb over the console and onto his lap, to let herself slide from fantasy into reality. She wanted to return the demands of his mouth, then simply sink in and not think at all.

The fingers on her neck slid up into her damp hair, and his thumb grazed the side of her jaw. Her skin tingled everywhere, and her breathing—well, maybe she'd stopped breathing, because her head was alive with sensations she couldn't hope to untangle.

The next thunderbolt vibrated the body of Eli's truck and shot straight up into her bones. Prying her mouth free, Sadie raised uncertain eyes. "Why do I feel like someone just reached down and gave us a really hard shake?"

"I thought it was my brain trying to shake some time-and-place sense into us."

Or sense in general, Sadie reflected. A sigh escaped as she forced her spinning emotions to disengage.

Did it surprise her that his kiss would be off the scale? Hardly. After one dance in Boston, she'd expected that scale to blow eventually.

It was an effort to separate herself from him and keep her voice steady. "This shouldn't have happened, Eli. We shouldn't have let it happen."

Skimming his knuckles over her cheekbone, he held her gaze. "I won't argue with you, but only because I know what I can and can't give a woman. More than sex is more than I've got inside me right now."

She laughed out a breath. "When I unscramble that remark, I'll probably agree. In the meantime…" She leaned forward just far enough to whisper a teasing "Your kisses rock, Lieutenant, with or without the drama of a full-blown storm beneath them."

Sadie knew he was considering tossing caution aside and diving in again, but he went with the wiser, if somewhat disappointing, alternative and reached behind them for his backpack. "It's time we put some distance between

us and these trees. Where's your—" he raised a humorous brow "—car?"

"Cars are neither bad words nor bad vehicles. I spent
half my teenage life wanting to own a Maserati."

"You own a Maserati?"

"No, I own a Land Rover, because I'm not in my teens,
and I knew when I came back to the Hollow that the roads,
in a pothole-to-pavement ratio, strongly favor the potholes.
My mother had a man friend once who leased a Maserati,
but I was thirteen when she left him, so I waved goodbye
to that wish and switched to boys instead."

"I didn't know your parents had broken up, Sadie. I'm
sorry."

She twitched away any residual sadness. "They were
barely together when we lived in the Hollow. Molly says
it's the Bellam curse."

"What is?"

"The inability of Nola Bellam's female descendants—
my mother in this case—to commit to people, places and/
or things. An inability she believes is supplemented by the
fact that those female descendants insist on passing the
Bellam surname on to their own female children."

"Would this be your cousin Molly who only left Raven's
Hollow long enough to go to college?"

"That's the one."

"Making her the notable exception commitment-wise."

"So it would seem."

With a smile grazing his lips, Eli indicated the outside
storm. "You ready?"

"Would saying no change the situation?"

His smile deepened. "Between lightning bolts, then."

He would be gorgeous, Sadie thought with a sigh. A hot,
gorgeous cop. A loner, with a reputation for getting the job
done—however distasteful that job might be.

As homicides went, Eli did it all. He'd go undercover for weeks, often months at a time, if going under meant bringing down a New York crime lord. During his tenure on the force, he'd worked countless night shifts while investigating gang-related murders. He'd hunted down serial killers, sunk his teeth into a dozen or more cold cases and, in at least one instance that she knew of, apprehended a man who made Hannibal Lecter appear well adjusted.

Of course, it also didn't hurt that he wore his dark hair long, always looked a little dangerous and somehow kept his truly superior six-foot-two-inch body totally cut.

"There's less than five seconds between thunderbolts," he said now. "We'll need to move fast and stay low."

"My way's better." Dragging her eyes from his profile, she regarded the storm-tossed trees. "Don't count, don't think, just do."

"Which is why, as a kid, you stepped in groundhog holes and sprained your ankles on a monthly basis."

"Two groundhog holes, two twisted ankles." And one dead hand, she recalled with a chill that she couldn't quite battle back. "On three?"

"Your count."

They exited the truck simultaneously. With her skirt tied into a thigh-baring knot, Sadie led the way to the narrowest part of the fallen tree's trunk. Before she could boost herself up and over, Eli scooped her off the ground.

"Wait, don't! Are you…" He deposited her without ceremony in a puddle on the far side. "…crazy?" she finished through her teeth.

Joining her, he shouldered his pack and grabbed her hand. "Come on."

Because arguing was pointless, Sadie ran with him to her Land Rover. They fell inside on the heels of a triple fork of lightning that illuminated the woodland hollow as far as she could see.

"Road's a single lane here." Raindrops flew from the ends of Eli's hair as he looked in several directions at once. "You're the DD, sweetheart. How are you at maneuvering in reverse?"

She summoned a tight smile. "Guess we'll find out."

Fortunately, she knew the twists and dips well enough to feel her way back through them. Eli's flashlight helped. So did the sky-wide slashes of lightning. Still, her nerves didn't stop jumping until they reached a point where the vehicle could be safely turned around.

"I'd say that was worthy of a Maserati should the opportunity for you to own one ever arise."

"Highly unlikely in this lifetime. And please don't say I could've had a fleet of them if I'd gone to New York, because everyone except my uncle—who looks on the *Chronicle* as a father might a beloved only child—has already pointed that out."

She felt more than saw his stare. "I get family loyalty, Sadie. You love your uncle, so you wanted to keep his dream alive. What I don't get is why he asked you to do it rather than someone who already lived in the Hollow."

"Back to Molly again, huh?"

"Rooney says she's smart, and given her history, I don't see her leaving town any time soon."

"She's an introvert, Eli."

"She worked at the *Chronicle* part-time through high school."

"As a proofreader. Look, I'm sure my uncle talked to her before approaching me. If Molly had wanted to run the newspaper, she'd be doing it." But she angled him an impressed look. "You've kept up, haven't you?"

"It's a hard loop to escape. There are six Blumes within

a six-block radius of my apartment. One of them lives across the street from me and drops by twice a week to make sure there's food in my fridge."

Sadie regarded the scattering of blackened houses as they approached Raven's Hollow. "Power's out. All I see are glimmers of light in a few… Stop it, Eli."

He hid most of a grin. "Stop what?"

"You're giving me a Molly smile. Those flickers are candles, not the spirits of Bellams past."

Now he chuckled. "I don't know, Sadie. Word has it Raven's Hollow was recently named one of three most haunted towns in New England."

"It was not." But she lowered suspicious lashes. "Who told you that?"

"Rooney."

"Well, in that case, consider the source. The man's propagating a myth to encourage tourism in the area."

"Always possible. One of my more ambitious cousins lived with him for a few years. He might have planted the thought. Does it bother you?"

Her lips curved into a deceptively sweet smile. "Do witches ride broomsticks?"

"I'll take the Fifth at this point. Something tells me you're only marginally tolerant when it comes to people who believe in the local lore."

"That's because I'm part of the local lore. Unfortunately."

She eased the Land Rover along a narrow, densely wooded road that wound up and up to a rocky promontory. The jagged point of land speared into a small bay where the waves, even on a calm day, broke white against the base of the cliff.

Built entirely of faded gray stone, Bellam Manor could at best be called forbidding. Although, Sadie mused, fore-

boding might be a more appropriate description. Either
way, two large towers stood at opposite ends of a struc-
ture made up of multiple juts and protrusions, and would
forever make her think of the wicked queen's castle from
Sleeping Beauty.

The mansion had taken fifteen years to construct. Sto-
rytellers swore that the evil secreted within the walls of
Blume House in Raven's Cove had nothing on this place.
But of course, Blume House had never been home to a
family of witches.

When she'd returned to the Hollow, Sadie had promised
herself she would do so with an open mind. The manor, as
remote as it was, and for all the tales that had been spun
around it, was simply a place to live. Or a small portion
of it was.

She had an apartment in one of the two habitable wings.
Molly occupied the second. It didn't take a structural en-
gineer to determine that the central core and several of the
outbuildings were in desperate need of restoration. Unfortunately, a full fix would take more money than she and
her cousin would earn in fifty years.

When a slash of lightning delineated the manor from
tower to imposing peak, she glanced over. "I'm waiting,
Lieutenant."

"Working on absorbing here, Sadie. I feel like we've
been swept off to the Black Forest by a freak tornado."

"That's how I felt when I saw the place again two years
ago. It was more of a fairy-tale castle when I was young,
but then I only came out here twice that I can remember."
She made a circular gesture. "My apartment backs onto
the ocean. Molly's overlooks the woods. It's an interesting
trek from my door to hers. Still no comment?"

"Still absorbing."

"Mmm, well, when you're done, I'll tell you that I'm not

eager to make the drive back down to town tonight, so I'm going to be generous and let you borrow my Land Rover."

Eli grinned. "Some would call that avoidance."

"My mistakes often have that result. For the most part, I circle around Ty the way Cocoa circles Molly's long-haired Chihuahua."

"Who's Cocoa?"

A dangerous smile appeared. "My cat. She's black. I've heard her referred to as my familiar. Ready?"

They waited through another flash of lightning, then made a dash for the porch. In the shelter of a wide over-hang, Sadie shoved the dripping hair from her face. "I could sit on a rock at the base of Bellam Point and not be this wet. Cocoa's going to think she scored a giant rat if she sees…me." When her eyes picked out an odd shadow, she bent forward to point. "Uh, Eli, can you shine your flashlight on that—whatever it is on my doorstep?"

He followed her gaze, frowned and, handing her the light, moved in for a closer look.

She clicked the switch. And immediately jerked back in disgust. "Oh, yuck. Dead bird. That's…" An ominous creak of hinges had her raising the beam slowly to the door. "…definitely not right."

Eli rose from his crouch. "Meaning you locked up this morning?"

"City girl. It's a habit." Her eyes traced the outline of the dark wooden frame. She honestly didn't know which was worse—the open door or the unfortunate creature lying outside it. Fighting a swell of fear that had already slicked her skin with ice, she said evenly, "What kind of sick person would put a dead raven on my welcome mat?"

"More to the point," Eli countered, "is that sick person waiting inside?"

Sadie's heart threatened to slam right out of her chest. "This is hell-and-gone creepier than my nightmares."

Already checking out the darkened entryway, Eli offered an absent "You have nightmares?"

She prodded his shoulder. "Later. There's a puddle of blood around the raven's head."

"Better its than yours. Stay behind me."

"Then keep moving. Dead animals are gross."

"Getting shot's grosser."

"Shot?" Astonishment halted her on the threshold. "Who'd want to shoot me?"

"You'd know that better than I would."

"It was a rhetorical question, Lieutenant. I'm not..."

A flurry of unexpected motion cut her off as someone leaped from the foyer shadows. Whoever it was knocked her into the doorframe, swung a lamp at Eli's head, then tossed it and bolted.

Trapping her arms, Eli stared into Sadie's slightly starry eyes. "Are you all right? Sadie, did he hurt you?"

"Yes—no." She willed the dizziness away. "I'm fine, I'm good. Go."

Cold metal brushed her wrist as he pulled a gun from the back of his jeans and vanished into the night.

Before she could turn, something swished across her calf. Swallowing a scream, she grabbed the discarded lamp and raised it like a bat.

A tiny meow floated upward from the floor.

"Cocoa..." Her breath rushed out in relief. "God."

She closed her eyes for a long moment, then, rubbing her head with the heel of her hand, retrieved the flashlight she'd dropped and pushed the door closed. When she touched the switch, a powerful beam of light bounced off the hall mirror and straight into her eyes.

"Oh, that was smart."

She needed another moment, she decided, to slow her spinning mind and regroup.

Three feathers on a door foreshadowed death in Raven's Cove. That was a matter of legend. She couldn't recall any mention of dead ravens on doorsteps in Raven's Hollow.

There had to be a crazy person on the loose.

But this didn't feel crazy, or not entirely. This was twisted and cruel and, when added to the email she'd received earlier, personal. It was…

The thought dissolved as she spied a slash of red on the wall opposite the mirror. The wall on which she was leaning!

Pushing off, she whirled in a half circle. And took three unbelieving steps back.

A single slashed word covered the plaster from end to end. It appeared to have been written by a giant claw. And said simply:

FOREVER!

Chapter Six

"Slow down. Let me get this straight." Sadie's former fiancé, Tyler Blume, gave her a light shake and sent Eli, several feet behind her, a fulminating look. "Someone broke into Bellam Manor, placed a dead raven on your doorstep and wrote a message in red on the wall. This person, who was still inside when you arrived, then proceeded to knock you down and fled the scene on foot with Eli in pursuit."

Sadie eased free of his increasingly tight grip. "Something like that, yes."

Ty's ice-blue eyes met the shadowed green of his cousin's. "I gather you lost him."

Eli's expression gave nothing away. "Unfortunately."

"So he was faster than you."

"Apparently."

"And smarter."

"If by that you mean he had a head start and a vehicle hidden in the woods, then yes, he was smarter."

"Were you able to obtain the license plate number of this hidden vehicle?"

"No."

"So all in all, your presence at the manor wasn't overly helpful."

Sadie drew her iPhone from her shoulder bag. "I didn't

come into town so you and your cousin could have a pissing contest, Ty."

"You shouldn't have come into town at all," he fired
back. "Why didn't you call me from the manor?"

She wagged her phone. "I did, three times. There was
no signal, and by the time I got one, we were in the Hollow." She made a frustrated gesture. "I heard the vehicle
Eli mentioned roar off."

"Direction?"

"East," Eli told him. "Toward Raven's Hollow."

A four-year stint in the army had taught Ty how to control his facial muscles, if not his entire expression.

"I'll need to inspect the site, gather more facts. You took
pictures of the bird and the wall. Kudos for that. But Eli
can't provide me with a license plate number, and neither
of you can describe the intruder, leaving me with nothing
except a dead raven, an eastbound vehicle and a single
painted word to go on."

"It was a truck." Eli kept his tone conversational.

Ty's dark blond eyebrows came together. "What was?"

"The eastbound vehicle. I'd guess a Dodge Ram,
twenty, maybe thirty years old. I'd also go with stolen
since the guy was smart enough to send the raven-card
email Sadie told you about from a toss-away phone." He
shrugged at his cousin's glare. "Police computer. I linked
to Sadie's office line. There's no owner registered on her
last incoming. Sender's got a plan, and it doesn't involve
being identified."

She'd known that, Sadie thought, of course she had.
She'd been a journalist far too long to delude herself. "I
don't suppose you have any idea, beyond terrifying me,
what that plan might entail?"

She felt Eli's gaze on her face. "Working on it."

Across the cramped room, Ty drummed a pen on his

blotter. "Tell me, cousin, how do you determine twenty or thirty years old in a truck?"

"Three back-breaking summers spent on my grandfather's farm in Idaho. Why are you wet?"

Ty frowned down at his soaked shirt and pants. "I—was hungry, stepped out. Figured the diner might be serving on emergency power."

"It's after eleven," Sadie remarked. "Johnny's closes at ten."

"The time thing didn't occur until I was halfway there. I was heading back when I spotted a couple kids outside Dorothy Leamer's antique store and made a detour."

Eli grinned. "Does she still keep her cash float in a cigar box under the counter?"

"It's her lucky box. She's been robbed a dozen or more times, but she always gets the money and the box back. Neither thing made it out of the store tonight. Unfortunately, the kids ran off before I could identify them."

"Making you and Eli even in the 'oops' department." Sadie indicated the curb outside. "The lamp the intruder used is in my Land Rover. I picked it up after he took off, but you could still check it for fingerprints."

A muscle in Ty's jaw ticked. "You figure there'll be any to find?" he asked Eli.

"Doubt it. You might get a clue from the bird. It was shot through the head."

"Did he use blood or paint for the wall message?"

"Paint. There wouldn't have been enough blood in a single raven to write a message that large."

"I assume you secured the scene."

"Do I really need to answer that?"

The tick in Ty's jaw deepened. "I think you should stay in town tonight, Sadie."

"And leave Molly alone out on the point? Answer's no."

"Fine." He yanked out his smartphone. "Is she at the manor?"

"Not when we were there. Save your battery, Ty. I've left five unanswered messages. All I can think of is that she went somewhere after work, turned her phone off and hasn't turned it back on yet."

"Right, then I'll just drive you home myself and spend the night.... Crap!" He scowled at his beeping cell, then breathed out and punched Talk. "Raven's Hollow Police Station. Chief Blume."

Leaving him to the call, Sadie joined Eli at the rain-streaked station window and studied his face. "Even in shadow, I can see the wheels turning. Talk to me, Lieutenant. Why would someone want to torment me with words that read like threats, and a raven with a bullet in its head?"

"*Mine forever.* Says it all, don't you think?"

She did, actually, or would have if she'd been willing to take it that far.

Ty's voice cut in. "Stay calm, Liz. I'll be right there." Frustration etched itself into his handsome features. "A six-year-old girl ran off in pursuit of her new puppy after it wiggled through a window. Now puppy and child are both lost. Mother's hysterical. Are you sure you secured the scene?" he demanded of Eli.

"I didn't ditch my badge and training at the state line. Everything you need to see will be there in the morning."

His cousin's response came in the form of a snarl. "See that it is." Giving Sadie's arm an awkward pat, he said, "Watch your back." Then he shot an accusing look in Eli's direction. "Unless you want a knife in it."

As soon as he was out the door, Sadie plastered a serene smile on her lips. "Well, that was horrible."

"Can I say I told you so?"

"Only if you want to walk to wherever it is you plan to sleep tonight."

"I was originally thinking Rooney's cottage."

"In that case, you're facing a long and treacherous hike."

He chuckled. "I haven't checked out the bulldog yet, Sadie. You know how Rooney gets stuck on a point."

"So…Ty's sofa it is. Good luck with that."

"Uh-huh." When she turned away, he tugged on her hair and swung her gently back around. "You know where I'll be sleeping tonight, and there won't be any old men, dogs or hostile sofas involved. Your front door lock's been compromised, Sadie."

Reaching behind her, Sadie extricated his hand from her hair. "You're trying to frighten me into letting you sleep at my place. Not only is that an unworthy tactic, it's also an unnecessary one, because while I don't appreciate your high-handed I'm-a-cop-and-you're-not attitude, I do in fact recognize that I've been threatened, and there was both a bullet and blood involved. So let's slide past the sleeping arrangements and the mind games, drive back to Bellam Manor and make sure Molly and Cocoa are safe."

The hand that had been in her hair moved to trap her chin. Eli's green eyes stared straight into hers. "This guy doesn't want Molly or Cocoa, Sadie. That's not what it's about."

She held his gaze. "What aren't you saying? I'm totally terrified to ask. In my experience, crazy people will steamroll anyone who gets in their way. Or so the theory generally goes."

"Generally," Eli agreed. "Except this isn't general, it's specific. And in terms of the email card you received, it's a virtual carbon copy of what happened to Laura a week before she was murdered."

TELLING SADIE WHAT had suddenly clicked in his mind did more than shock her into silence. It catapulted Eli back to the night his stepsister—Sadie's seventeen-year-old cousin, Laura—had died.

Sadie's aunt had married Eli's widowed father when Eli was ten. The melding of their families had been a seamless affair. But no doubt about it, Bellams and Blumes living under the same roof in Raven's Cove had been like Christmas on the local grapevine.

Eli and two friends from school had gone to a movie in the Cove the night of the murder. Laura had been babysitting Sadie, but she'd driven to the Hollow in her mother's cherry-red '69 Mustang with a promise to pick them up as soon as her aunt and uncle returned home.

He could have told her not to bother, Eli thought now. Less of a hassle to walk or let someone closer come and get them, but there'd been intermittent hailstorms all day, and face it, what adolescent boy would turn down a ride in the coolest car in town?

So he and his friends had wandered over to the arcade to wait. They'd slain dragons, bludgeoned knights and smashed castle walls, until, finally, the manager had come in and told them he was shutting down.

Eli had felt the first prickle of fear at that moment. He hadn't known why, not exactly. It hadn't been until later that he'd remembered hearing Laura on the phone three days earlier, pleading with someone to stop pestering her.

Drama queen, he'd figured at the time. People called Laura a diva, and, what the hell, she'd stuck her tongue out at the handset after slamming it down, so how serious could the call have been?

He'd gotten his answer that weekend when, feeling sick and guilty, he'd trudged into the hollow to search for her. Everyone had been looking by then, yet oddly enough, the only person he'd bumped into in the dense woods was Sadie.

He'd known something was terribly wrong, because he'd snuck into Laura's room and discovered a card with two ravens on it in the wastepaper basket under her desk. She'd torn it up, but the pieces had been easily reassembled, and once whole, had made even a fourteen-year-old boy's blood run cold.

The scrawl inside had read MY LOVE in bold red letters. There'd been no signature, and of course, nothing on or in it could be traced. Not to the boyfriend Laura had recently broken up with or to anyone in the Cove or the Hollow.

But someone had written those words. Someone who'd either sent the card or slipped it to her before she'd died. Someone, Eli reflected darkly, who'd sent Sadie an eerily similar message—two full decades later.

SADIE LET HIM drive her Land Rover up the treacherous road to Bellam Manor. They didn't talk much, which was normal enough for Eli and perfectly fine with her. Staving off terror took concentration and strong mental locks.

Two ravens, though, on two separate cards, two decades apart. One imprisoned, one free. And no signature in either case.

Determined not to think about where this was leading, she attempted to contact Molly again. But her cousin's voice mail picked up, and as it did, frustration slipped past the knot of fear in her throat. She turned in her seat. "Why didn't I hear about Laura's card before tonight, Eli? Or the phone call you say she got?"

He kept his eyes on the road and his tone mild. "You were seven years old. You found her body in Raven's Bog. Literally tripped on her hand and went down. The doctors in both the Hollow and the Cove agreed you must be in shock. And I repeat—only seven."

"A resilient seven." She tapped an impatient thumbnail on her phone. "The only call I've gotten came in conjunction with the email that was sent to me today at the *Chronicle*."

"Still a call."

She thought back. "The voice was computer altered. I didn't recognize it."

"Male?"

"Inasmuch as a synthesized voice can have a gender, yes. In any case, the intruder at the manor was male. And don't you dare suggest an accomplice. This is twisted enough already. Whoever hit Laura with a tire iron left her and her car in what used to be the heart of the hollow. But twenty years ago, the road we were on tonight—which is the only drivable road from end to end—was nothing more than a goat path. So, obvious next question. How did her car wind up in the bog?"

"The consensus was that Laura let the killer get into the car. Once inside, he forced her to drive to Raven's Bog. They exited the car, he struck her, then left her body, the Mustang and the murder weapon at the scene."

"Do you know where the tire iron came from?"

"An auto scrap yard in Bangor."

"So, summing up, there were no fingerprints on the murder weapon, there was no blood in the car and nothing but… God, why am I doing this?" Unbelieving, Sadie drilled her index fingers into her temples. "It's insane, like Laura's murderer—who's apparently been in the area all along. Whoever he is, this guy's a volcanic time bomb on a really slow tick. And he seems to have it in for Bellam females." When Eli didn't respond, she lowered her hands.

"A little reassurance would be nice here, Lieutenant—before I totally freak out!"

He made the final turn to the manor. "Would it help if I said we could be dealing with a copycat?"

"Which would be better—how exactly?"

"Different perpetrator, potentially different…motive."

She pounced. "You hesitated before you said 'motive.'"

"I hesitated because something just blew off one of the manor's towers and across my line of vision."

"You were going to say 'outcome,' weren't you? Potentially different outcome. As in he might shoot me instead of using a tire iron."

"Sadie…"

"I know." She went back to pushing on her temples. "Freaking myself out again. I need to refocus, and lucky me, I see a light in Molly's window. I can distract myself by reading her the riot act for turning off her phone."

"Isn't shouting at Molly a bit like kicking a puppy?"

"I said read, not shout. All I really want to do is make sure she's safe. Because I don't believe, and neither do you, that there's a copycat at work here. It's twenty years later, Eli, and somebody's doing to me almost exactly what he did to Laura. But who's to say that after such a long hiatus, this person doesn't have a different plan in mind? How do we know I'm the only Bellam he intends to threaten? Or kill?"

HE SAT IN the dark, with the storm shrieking around him, and he breathed. In and out, in and out.

It was all about making the right moves at the right time. He wanted Sadie. He needed Sadie to know he wanted her. But he also needed her to know she'd hurt him.

Love and fear and anger fought a bitter, three-way battle in his head these days. Twenty years ago, he'd discovered that a sleeping monster lived deep inside him. What if the monster woke up and consumed him? He might kill Sadie the way he'd killed Laura.

Would he, though? Could he? He loved Sadie so very, very much. He saw himself spending the rest of his life with her. Was it possible this newer, deeper love might stop the monster from clawing its way out?

Possibly, but one thing he'd learned tonight was that accidents could happen when you carried a gun.

The raven should have been a symbol of his love. He hadn't meant to kill it, but at least the bullet hadn't wound up in Sadie's head. He could take comfort in that.

When he started to shake, he dropped his face into his hands. He was tired, so damnably tired. Should he try to sleep? Did he dare? Or would the monster know and seize the opportunity to go on a rampage?

To go on a witch-hunt?

Chapter Seven

"The battery in her cell phone died."

Twenty minutes after they walked through her cousin's front door. Sadie returned to the thickly shadowed room Molly called a parlor.

"She stayed in town to have dinner with a friend who's afraid of thunderstorms. Neat, tidy, logical. Mystery solved, Lieutenant."

"One mystery, anyway." Eli held up and examined a double-edged dagger. "Any reason she collects and displays lethal weapons?"

"Witch's tools," Sadie corrected. "That dagger you're holding is an athame. Its white-handled counterpart is a boline." She swept a hand along the sideboard. "Chalice, ritual candles, tarot cards, protective crystals—dog."

Eli regarded the tiny, ratlike creature at the far end. Its pointy ears quivered as the animal stared back.

"His name's Solomon." Sadie bit back most of a smile. "He and Cocoa don't get along. Seeing as Molly's coming with us to my place, it should be a lively gathering."

"Especially if Cocoa's in the mood for a midnight snack."

"I'll make sure she's well fed. By the way, you might want to put that dagger down before Molly sees you. She's proprietorial about family heirlooms."

"Seriously? These things belonged to your ancestor?"

"Most of them did. Molly's a buff. She's searched the manor from subcellar to tower peak. If you look closely, you'll see Nola Bellam's initials inscribed on the larger items."

"So Hezekiah Blume really did marry a witch."

"Depends on how you look at it. Nola possessed the implements of a witch, but then Molly currently possesses those same implements, and no one's ever accused her of witchcraft."

"I'll let that one pass."

"And I'll light a metaphorical fire under my cousin." But Sadie paused in the doorway. "Do you have any ideas, theories, even vague thoughts on tonight's intruder?"

"Having seen this house, I'd say he doesn't believe in curses."

"Oh, well, if that's true, you can take almost every male in both towns out of the running."

"There you go. Should be an easy solve."

"Five minutes." Giving the molding a double tap, she left Eli alone with the lash of rain and wind outside and a tangle of thoughts in his head.

He was a cop, he reminded himself. Solid facts and cold, hard evidence were his life. What was screwing it all up for him at the moment was his inability to slam a mental door on the welter of Sadie-related emotions he didn't want to feel.

She'd been a beautiful child, with her wild mass of red-brown hair and her amazing storm-gray eyes. Fortunately, back then—kid. Unfortunately, now—woman.

His own eyes shifted as wind whipped through cracks in the ceiling and rattled the window glass.

"No one's going to rob you, Molly." Sadie returned a

few minutes later with her cousin in tow. "And the more people under one roof tonight, the better."

Yes, no, maybe. Eli managed not to grind his teeth as he watched Sadie bend to pick up her black trench coat. "Could you bring Solomon?" Her expression solemn, Molly dragged her Bellam red hair into a ponytail. "He doesn't bite."

Did he even have teeth? But Eli tucked the dog under his arm and followed the women into the storm.

Confusion reigned from the moment they entered Sadie's plant-filled home. As predicted, Cocoa chased the Chihuahua under a tall cabinet. The lights flared and died three times, and in spite of the fact that he'd draped a sheet over the sinister message, on one of his trips through the foyer, he found Molly easing a corner up for a look.

"Morbid curiosity?" he inquired from the shadows.

She jumped back a full foot before finding him in the dark. "I was just—I wanted to see. It's not that I don't believe what Sadie said, I'm only surprised anyone would come into Bellam Manor to do it. A lot of people are afraid of this place."

"But not you."

"No. I mean—why would I be?" She touched her ponytail. "The house wouldn't turn on one of its own."

Okay, that was weird. But, as he recalled, so was Molly. Or had been back when he'd lived in the Cove.

With a small smile, she and her flickering candle more or less melted into the darkness. Unsure what to make of her, Eli checked the writing behind the sheet, listened to the storm for another moment, then made his way to the kitchen.

He saw Cocoa sitting calmly on the windowsill while Sadie rummaged in a high cupboard. "No offense," he said genially, "but your cousin hasn't gotten any less strange with time."

"I've heard that before. Yet people keep coming into the pharmacy to have their prescriptions filled. Not to worry, her plan for the rest of the night is to lock herself in my guest room with her tarot cards, her laptop and, I'm pretty sure, since it appears to be missing, my grandmother's carving knife."

Eli straddled a hard chair while she continued to rummage. "Am I responsible for that, or does Molly generally sleep with knives?"

"I think you unsettle her."

"Makes us even."

Sadie laughed, and the sound of it was a punch of pure lust in his gut. "You are not afraid of my cousin, Eli."

"No? I heard a story in my junior year. A girl who humiliated her wound up with a bad case of warts."

"Where do you get this stuff? Never mind." She held up a hand. "Rooney. Ah, good, found them." She set a taper and three pillar candles on the table. "Your great-grandfather is leaning as heavily on our witchy legend as he is on the Raven's Tale in order to entice tourists to visit *your* town."

Warily fascinated, Eli tracked her movements. "Nola Bellam married Hezekiah Blume, Sadie. That's a fact. The legends are intertwined and fair game for anyone wanting to use them as an enticement."

She aimed the taper at him. "This is why my great-grandfather went to live in the north woods."

Sadie had a hypnotic way of moving, Eli noted. By the glow of a single taper, she appeared to float around the kitchen. Her still-damp tank top and skirt clung to her in a way that made his lower body burn and brought him right to the edge of begging.

Common sense and a hard slap of memory would keep those reactions in check, but it would still take every scrap of restraint he possessed not to jump her.

When he realized she was watching him, he shrugged off her last remark. "You want to talk fear factor, your great-grandfather's got it all over Rooney. What is he now, ninety-five?"

"Ninety-nine." Sweeping around behind him, she ran a teasing finger over his hair. "Hot on Rooney's colorful heels."

With a silent curse, Eli caught her hand. Coming smoothly to his feet, he murmured, "This sleepover thing actually might not be such a good idea. We're standing here talking about weird cousins and Hezekiah, a man people think is a ghost, and what I'm really wondering is why the hell we're talking at all."

She resisted ever so slightly as he drew her toward him. "We agreed back at your truck not to do this."

"I remember the conversation." He held her gaze. "And you can stop me any time. We both know there's nowhere for it to go. Cops and relationships don't work. Trust me, I've been there and back again."

With his thumb and fingers, he captured her chin, tipping her head up until he saw the glimmer in her eyes. He recognized the challenge in them, but right then he didn't care. He wanted his mouth on hers, and screw the consequences. The moment for any last chance objections came and went as he brought her lips slowly up to meet his.

He'd keep it brief, he promised himself, hot and fast, a flash of desire satisfied.

It would have worked if she'd been another woman. Any woman other than the one he'd met and danced with in Boston.

Her fingers curled into his hair, and she moved against

him in a kind of sinuous samba. He let his hands roam over her ribs, then around them so his palms cupped her breasts. He breathed in the scent of her while his tongue explored her mouth. She smelled like wild roses. She tasted like sin. She felt like the answer to a prayer.

If there were answers.

If he'd had prayers.

Easing back a tempting inch, she regarded him through her lashes. "I can feel the conflict in you, Eli. I know what it's like to want but know you can't or shouldn't have. I think."

"That's part of our problem, isn't it?" His eyes traveled over her face. "We're always thinking."

Her smile widened. "Not sure I'd say that, Lieutenant." And yanking his mouth back down onto hers, she blasted everything that didn't have its roots in need from his head.

It might have been lightning or the glow from the taper that caused the darkness to shift. Whatever the source, when he spotted a shadow that shouldn't be there, his body stilled.

Sensing the change, Sadie drew back. "What is it?"

"Not sure." He scanned the spread of black rocks that led to the edge of the cliff. "No, don't look." He held her in place when she started to turn. "Pretend we're talking."

"We are talking." But she gave the ends of his hair a playful flick with one hand, and skimmed the fingers of her other across his cheek. "What do you see?"

He kissed her forehead. "Unless Molly's taking a late night stroll, someone's out there."

"Wonderful. Can you tell if 'someone's' carrying a gun?"

"I'll need more than a glimpse for that. The light's pretty much nonexistent."

"I am so getting a generator."

Ten seconds ticked by. "There it is." He drew his own gun from the back of his jeans. "Considering its remote location, Bellam Manor's a busy place tonight. Is there a side door?"

"Through the pantry. Eli, are you sure...?"

"Dead raven," he reminded her, and she held up her hands in surrender.

A feeble streak of lightning flashed as the storm limped grudgingly out to sea. With his gun pointed skyward, and his eyes alert, Eli inched the pantry door open, waited a beat, then stepped out into the gusting rain.

"Come on," he muttered to the shadowy caller. "Give me a target."

He got one ten seconds later in the form of a barely there movement that indicated the caller was creeping along the back of the house.

Whoever it was wore a long coat and had one hand pressed to the outer wall. The other hand—he couldn't tell. Might be carrying a weapon, might be holding something else. Like another dead bird?

Able to just make out the flat rocks ahead, he jammed the gun in his waistband and went for a takedown. When the shadow lost its balance on the slippery ground, Eli knew it was over.

One solid tackle was all it took. Surprised by the ease of the capture, rather than plant a knee, he flipped his quarry over. And found himself face-to-face with a writhing, swearing female.

Even fully pinned, she bucked, thrashed and squirmed, twisting her head from side to side. At length, she settled for spitting at him.

"Stop fighting me," he shouted above the wind. "I don't want to hurt you."

She either didn't hear him or didn't care, and spat again.

Cursing now, Eli released her left hand. It flew straight up toward his face, but he blocked the blow with his elbow and snatched her hood back.

Bared teeth and furious eyes greeted him. In that same split second, she succeeded in freeing a knee and immediately aimed at his groin.

"Not tonight, lady." He knocked it off to the side. "Who the hell are you?"

She tried to heave him up and off. "None of your business. Get—off—me!"

They shot wildcats in Maine, didn't they? "Calm down," he said again. "I'm a cop."

"Screw that, pal. I know Ty Blume and his deputies. You're not one of them."

Firming his hold on her wrists, he focused on her face. "You know Ty?"

It didn't surprise him when Sadie dropped down beside him and squeezed his arm. "She knows Ty, Eli. And I know her. You can let her go, but do it carefully. She has a spiteful temper."

The female snorted. "Pot, kettle, Sadie."

"We mostly tolerate each other," Sadie continued in an unruffled tone. "You remember my cousin, Orley, Eli. She's a veterinary assistant by day and, I'll assume, Ty's watchdog by night." Nudging his shoulder, she added an amused "Good thing you know your job, Lieutenant, because Orley here is also a former state champion in mixed martial arts."

Chapter Eight

"We've been over this, Sadie," her cousin maintained the following morning. "Yes, Ty sent me. But the word 'spy' never came up."

"Implied's as good as stated."

Arms folded, Orley slumped down in the passenger seat. "The guy was worried about you. He couldn't leave the station house, and he couldn't get through to Deadbeat Molly, so he called and asked me to spend the night at the manor. Easy breezy."

"There's no easy in Ty's world." Sadie shoved her four-by-four into a lower gear for the descent to Ben Leamer's farm. "He didn't want me to be alone with Eli, and he had no idea if and or when Molly might show. Solution? Recruit a stand-in."

Orley thrust up her bruised forearms. "You're bitching, but I'm the one who got mowed down and pinned by Officer Sexy."

"Lieutenant Sexy," Sadie shot back, then made a growling sound. "If you think Eli's so hot, why aren't you with him instead of me? A tow truck was waiting with a new tire when we dropped him off at the fallen pine."

Her cousin snorted. "News bulletin, sunshine. The über-hot Lieutenant Blume only has eyes for you. He also only didn't insist on going with you to Ben's farm because he needs his truck back, and I'd already agreed to ride shot-gun. He might have liked it better if Molly had done the honors, but her being totally anal and all, that wasn't going to happen. The pharmacy must be unlocked precisely at eight a.m. She has OCD, you know. Undiagnosed, but even you can't deny she's peculiar, and getting worse every day."

Amusement rose as Sadie spied the farm. "I can deny a lot of things, actually. It's the curse—or the gift, your choice—of a vivid imagination."

"Do not use the word 'curse' in any conversation that involves Molly. If it pertains to the Cove or the Hollow, it's under an evil spell as far as she's concerned. Now, using that as our segue, talk to me about the messages you've received."

Sadie pulled into the driveway and, with the park brake set, regarded the sky. Angry black clouds threatened an-other deluge, but so far so dry. "I know you love ghoulish details, Orley, but I've given you all there are, so bury your curiosity and back off. I have pictures to take of what I'm told is a truly spooky corn maze."

Her cousin made a dubious face at the high field of corn that spread out forever from the side of a secondary barn. "The maze is an okay deal, but the rest of Leamer's farm creeps me out. Animals die, you cremate or bury them. You do not set up a side business to stuff them for people who are as icky-minded as you are."

"I'm not here to watch Ben preserve someone's dead pet. Getting lost in a cornfield has snowballed into a pop-ular October event. Kids love it."

"Kids are easy marks."

Sadie grinned. "You weren't."

"Neither were you. Face it, kid, we're Bellams. Nobody expects us to be normal."

"Then why do you have a problem with Molly?"

Hopping out, Orley zipped her coat. "Partly because she and I are both a few years shy of forty, and while I can see her not being married, I haven't figured out why it's never happened for me. I'm not an anal fusspot that people avoid because they're afraid they'll wake up with a face full of warts." She blew at her long red bangs. "That sounds small-minded and mean, doesn't it?"

"A little."

"Do you understand why?"

"Because Molly was a straight-A student, and you weren't?"

"Well, hold the phone, cousin—neither were you."

Sadie regarded her over the Land Rover's roof. "How did this get to be about me?"

"It didn't. It isn't. I just can't figure Molly, and I hate it when people compare me to her. She's a freak, even by Bellam standards."

"She's an introvert, Orley, but before we bite each other's heads off over this, let's change the subject. Otherwise, you'll challenge me to a kickboxing match where I'm sure to wind up on my butt, in what I hope, but seriously doubt, is mud."

"Awkward sentence, excellent call."

After tugging a short red jacket over her T-shirt and jeans, Sadie crawled into the backseat to hunt through her camera bag. When her cousin didn't speak, she rolled her eyes. "I can feel your curiosity from here." Crawling back out, she looked around. "Come on, Ben, I haven't got all day.... And no, Orley, we didn't have sex."

Her cousin strolled closer, smirking. "Does that mean he's a lousy kisser?"

Sadie sent her a guileless smile. "If you mean Ben Leamer, I wouldn't know. If you mean Eli, it's none of your business."

"Why not? You're a public figure, he's a public figure."

"Eli defends the public, he's not a figure of it."

"Public's public. Also please note, I said kiss, not sex."

"You're working up to sex. And what makes you think I've kissed him—as if I can't guess?"

"You have a big kitchen window. No blinds, easy pickup."

"Yeah, for anyone creeping around the manor." Sadie made a shooing motion with her fingers. "Creep over to the maze entrance, will you? I need a point of reference."

Orley's shoulders hunched. "I don't like having my picture taken. And I wasn't creeping. I didn't get an answer at the front door, so I went around to the back, and there you both were, getting hot and bothered in the kitchen. Being a considerate sort, I opted to retrace my steps to the front. You saw how it went from there. FYI, your sexy lieutenant's very strong."

"Know it." Sadie crouched for a better angle. "Move left."

"I'm freezing. Where did the stupid heat go?"

"South. Stop fidgeting."

Her cousin snarled out a breath. "Any chance we'll be done by noon? Brady and I are supposed to do a dental on a Doberman—assuming the road to the Cove gets cleared and he makes it to the clinic with the anesthetic we have almost none of. While we're on the topic, have you thought about...?"

"Adding a veterinary procedure of the month column to the *Chronicle?* You've asked me that twenty times already."

"Animals are cute, Sadie."

"Animals are adorable. Procedures aren't. Will you please stand still?"

"I'm cold. I'm also trying to normal things up around

here. People are talking, and not just about Rooney Blume's birthday."

A chill that had nothing to do with the dipping temperature skated along Sadie's spine. "I don't want to talk about Laura."

"Neither do I. I was referring to the Hezekiah Blume, Nola Bellam story."

"Legend." Sadie snapped three quick shots. "Based on historical fact."

"Fictionalized fact."

"Only certain aspects. A record of the marriage between Hezekiah Blume and Nola Bellam exists. We also know, via the family Bible, that the union pissed off Hezekiah's brother, Ezekiel, to the point that Ezekiel got drunk and raped Nola while Hezekiah was out of town."

"What a sweetheart," Orley muttered.

"Yeah, really sweet. To cover his butt, little brother branded Nola a witch—not a difficult thing to do given the strange nature of her family and the grim state of the Hollow in those days—whereupon, he and several fearful residents of Raven's Cove proceeded to hunt her down in the woods. He thought he killed her, but, oops, he missed." Sadie adjusted her camera lens. "When he returned to the Cove, Hezekiah, also believing Nola was dead, went on a rampage and murdered not only Ezekiel but every one of the townspeople who'd been involved in the hunt."

"After which—enter fiction." Orley wiggled her fingers. "Hezekiah recanted the evil spirit he'd taken into himself, and was ultimately transformed into a raven. The whole witch thing might have faded into folklore if Nola hadn't popped up again or, as the locals saw it, returned from the dead."

"That was just her outsmarting Ezekiel and his nasty compatriots."

"Ezekiel loved Nola, Sadie. He was willing to take her daughter as his own. And don't forget he met her before she and Hezekiah ever laid eyes on each other."

"Meaning what? First come, first served? Nola was in love with Hezekiah and vice versa. The order of meeting is irrelevant."

"Little bro was head over heels. From his perspective, big bro screwed him around. Guy went a little crazy is all."

"Right, because witch-hunts are only a *little* crazy." Sadie's gaze touched on a pair of rusted-out tractors and a wooden plow from the early twentieth century. "Doesn't look like Ben's going to show, does it?"

"Nope, ergo he must have had one whopping big emergency, because he was strutting around the Hollow yesterday, pleased as punch, telling anyone who'd listen that his corn maze would be getting a full page spread in next Sunday's edition." Blowing on her balled hands, Orley moved away from the entrance. "You know, Sadie, with all this talk about Hezekiah, Ezekiel and Nola, it occurs to me that you and Eli and Ty have a kind of parallel story happening here. Except you don't have a daughter, and Nola did."

"And Ezekiel was insane, and Ty isn't. Not to mention that Eli wouldn't turn to the dark side and wind up damned no matter what the inducement. Otherwise, though, absolutely, parallel story."

"It was an idle observation, cous. Tell me we're ditching this spook farm, and I'll zip it."

"We'll leave." Sadie grinned at her. "Right after I try out the maze."

"Damn, I knew you were going to say that."

"You can play with my iPad in the Rover. It shouldn't take me more than twenty minutes to work my way through."

"Okay, but word of caution. Ben's got jumping things

in there. Scarecrows and ravens, and pitchforks and supersized spiders that drop from webs."

"Consider me warned."

She'd have done this in any case, Sadie thought, but with Orley determined to explore in detail a legend that had haunted her sleeping mind for more than a week, the idea of getting lost in a cornfield took on added appeal.

They hadn't been close as children. Orley, Molly and Laura had all been a full decade older than her. And with her parents' marriage being about as crappy as it got, family gatherings had been few and far between.

The child she'd been hadn't thought much about the lack of contact with her relatives—until her aunt Cordelia had married Eli's father. Then she'd paid attention. Because little girls developed big crushes. And she'd tumbled hard for dark-haired, green-eyed Eli Blume.

Had it ever worn off? she wondered, as she pushed through the rustling stalks. Difficult to say, but her dreams had certainly taken on a different flavor with Eli at the manor last night. The tension inside her had been less bloodcurdling and more sensual. Which might mean that her heart was in as much danger as her life.

As Nola's had been when she'd chosen Hezekiah over Ezekiel?

Don't go there, Sadie, a voice in her head ordered. Far less terrifying to think about Eli's kisses than the dead bird on her doorstep. And better not to do either thing since navigating the maze required more than a little concentration.

She dead-ended twice and had to backtrack to forks that arrowed off in multiple directions. Ravens circling overhead emitted rough, taunting caws. The wind whistled eerily through the stalks. And, as Orley had predicted, all manner of things jumped out at her.

She made it past the swinging brooms easily enough, but gritted her teeth when a spider the size of a dinner plate dropped down five inches from her face. Half a step later, its eight-legged mate shot down to join it.

Okay, arachnids were definitely worth a pause.

With the tarantulas on steroids still bobbing in the breeze, Sadie glanced back down the path. It wasn't fair to blame Ben Leamer for the raw state of her nerves, but even setting that aside, she thought this portion of the maze might be a little too realistic for kids under ten. Not being under ten herself, however, she told the spiders to smile and snapped a close-up shot.

Did she only imagine the tarantulas were leering at her through the lens?

"Get a grip, Sadie," she muttered, and pushed past the pair of them.

She chose her next path at random. A scarecrow holding a wooden ax leaped out as she rounded a corner. She handled that one, but when a much nastier version burst out ten steps later, a laughing scream escaped.

Score one for Ben, she decided, and proceeded with greater care. So what if fat drops of rain were beginning to plop on the stalks? Unless it flooded the maze, a little water wouldn't hurt her.

Neither would a human-sized raven wearing a black cloak, but having one swoop into sight while she was glancing skyward sent her heart into her throat and stopped her in her tracks.

"Okay." She said it slowly, then took a moment to gather her wits. "Hezekiah Blume, I presume." Red eyes shone from the folds of a bulky hood. "Did not see you coming at all." Releasing a cautious breath, she lowered her gaze.

And spied an envelope fastened to the front of his cloak. Everything inside her turned to liquid. But that was an automatic first response. Her second was to spin in a stationary circle. "You are not going to frighten me." She kept her voice even and her senses alert. "I won't let you." Then a twig snapped directly behind her and her muscles went rigid. She whirled, blew out a breath. "Jesus— Orley."

"Yes, Orley. Who did you think?" Clearly out of sorts, her cousin brushed at her coat and short hair. "I felt like a coward sitting in your Jeep, plus Ben's hired hand showed up, and I did not want to hear about his six and a half kids, so I sucked it up and followed you. All was well until a damn bat attacked me in one of the…" When her eyes locked on the envelope, her voice trailed off. "What's that? No, sorry, obvious answer. But—" she ticked a finger "—don't think I'm liking the white thing with your name on it."

"Tell me about it."

Although she would have preferred to burn the envelope, Sadie yanked it free and ran her thumbnail along the sealed flap.

Inside she discovered a card with a jagged red heart just beginning to crack. "Hell," she whispered. And bracing for the worst, opened it.

While I love, the monster sleeps.

Orley offered a breathy "Holy crap" while Sadie reread the fractured scrawl.

When several wet drops of rain landed on her head, she shot a dangerous look at the clouds. "Stop raining!"

Orley stabbed a finger. "That is a gonna-get-you threat, Sadie."

"I know what it is."

She also knew—though she wasn't sure how she heard it over the roar of blood in her head—that her phone was ringing.

With the card and envelope in one hand, she slid the fingers of her other into her jeans pocket.

Orley read the screen over her shoulder. "Bob's Cleaning Service?"

Eyes still fixed on the effigy, Sadie hit Speaker. "What is it, Bobby?"

"So sorry, my love, but I borrowed your janitor's phone."

The computer voice hit her like a physical blow—until she pictured the gray-haired cleaning man who'd given her gumdrops as a child. "Where's Bobby?" she demanded, ignoring Orley's attempts to mime a message. "What have you done to him?"

"I don't hurt old men, Sadie. I simply borrowed—well, stole—his phone." A long pause preceded a raspy "I know you got my message."

Sadie executed a warier circle this time. "Which one?"

"The card with the heart."

He was here, she realized. He was watching.

A sudden horrible thought occurred. "Where's Ben Leamer?"

"Sleeping. Soundly."

"You knew I'd go into the maze when he didn't show."

"Hoped," the caller replied. "Saw. Used the opportunity."

"How long have you been following me?"

"Long enough to know you're not...alone."

Orley's fingernails bit into her arm. "We need to get out of here."

Still searching the stalks, Sadie managed a steady "What do you want me to do?"

Even disguised, the unexpected pain came through. "I want you not to break my heart. I want you to care. I want you to please, please not wake the monster!"

Chapter Nine

By Eli's estimation, less than a quarter of his attention was focused on the task at hand. Not the ideal scenario for someone using a chain saw to cut up a fallen tree.

His cousin Brady, who operated the Raven's Hollow Veterinary Clinic, had come and gone three times in the past two hours. Each time he reappeared, he had a more powerful saw in the back of his battered Ford truck.

"This could be the best cutter in the county." Hopping up into the box, he shifted the tool so Eli could view the massive blade. "Problem is, Paul Bunyan's not here to operate it, and I've never used anything this big before."

The tow truck driver, a beefy man with nervous eyes, slapped his gloves on his thigh. "Might be two could lift the thing. Eli?"

"Pass. I'm not eager to hack off a foot. Midsized version works for me."

Brady hunkered down. "What we need is a plow horse."

"What we need is an ox." With all four of his wheels intact, Eli tossed a chain around a freshly cut section of pine and fastened it to his winch. "All we have to do until the road crew arrives is make an opening wide enough for an emergency vehicle to get through."

The driver from Cove Towing made an anxious sweep of the woods. "Not sure I wanna picture emergency vehicles when I'm standing in the middle of the hollow. Lots of folks hereabouts swear this is a haunted place, and near the bog most of all."

Eli tugged on the chain to secure it. "You're letting Rooney's wild stories get to you, Brick."

"Nothing wild about your stepsister's death. A believer would say there's possession involved. The guy she dumped two weeks before had Blume blood."

Brady glanced at Eli. "The guy she dumped also had an alibi for the time of the murder."

"Yeah, but who gave him that alibi? His own ma, that's who."

Rain began to spit from a nasty-looking sky. Eli figured they'd be soaked in a minute whether he pursued this or not. "Her ex's name was Cal Kilgore, Brick." He turned to his cousin. "Is Cal still in the Cove?"

"More out than in," Brady told him. "He built a cabin in the north woods and got himself a forge. Last I heard, he was making specialized metal products and selling them to a wholesale outfit in Bangor."

"How often do you see him?"

"Three times in the last fifteen years. And not much more than that before he left town. He was older than Laura by about five years, so that'd put him around forty-two these days."

Interesting, Eli reflected. Not necessarily relevant, but worth a back-check.

He heard a squawk from the tow truck, which signified an incoming call, and noted the instant expression of relief on Brick's face. "Looks like we're about to lose some of our muscle."

Dragging on a rumpled jacket, Brady grinned. "Happens a lot in this spot." He nodded at the tree. "You can tell me to mind my own, but seeing as your truck was stuck on the Cove side, how is it you wound up spending the night in the Hollow?"

Eli drew off his work gloves. "It's a long story. Short version, I hitched a ride with Sadie."

His cousin's brown eyes registered surprise. "Sadie was out on this spit-slick road in last night's storm? Why?"

"She got a crank call at the newspaper. It pissed her off."

"That'd make sense if Ty's office wasn't in exactly the opposite direction from the one she must have been taking."

"Think it through, Brady."

"Just did. Clever avoidance of an ex." He sighed when Brick waved an arm out his window and roared off. "As predicted, there goes a third of our muscle. Do you hear a siren?"

"Yep."

Brady tucked his wire-rimmed reading glasses inside the jacket and murmured a semi-amused "Let the fireworks begin."

With his more ornery cousin still a good distance away, Eli returned to his truck and used its mechanical muscle to drag a large branch off the road.

The prospect of a second confrontation with Ty didn't bother him. But spending the better part of the morning with his mind caught between a threat and a kiss? That just plain sucked. It also irritated him that not one but both things scared the hell out of him.

He'd tried for a relationship once, with an entertainment journalist…and where in hell had that disaster of a memory crawled in from? She'd messed up; then he'd messed up, and they'd both paid the price for it. End of nightmare.

Eli squeezed his truck through the new opening and was prepping the chain again when Ty squealed to a halt.

Surly and spoiling, he strode over to plant his booted feet less than eighteen inches from where his cousin crouched.

"Problem?" Eli asked, not looking up.

"You didn't leave the damn bird."

"Yeah? Where was I supposed to leave the damn bird, Ty? On your desk in an unlocked police station?"

"Raven's Hollow isn't the back of beyond. We have an evidence room with an automatic lock."

"Right." Now he looked up. "Did you expect me to shoot out the lock to gain access to the room? You left before us, Chief, and street-entrance dead bolts only work with keys—which I didn't have. Next accusation?"

Ty widened his stance. "Do you want it in the face or the stomach?"

Perfect, Eli thought, and stood. "You want to fight me? Here? Now?"

"What he wants," Brady put in from a wise distance, "is a free shot. My advice? Take it in the stomach. He's got a tricky uppercut."

Rain had begun to dribble past the collar of Eli's jacket. That, combined with a petulant wind and his deteriorating mood, made the prospect of a good fistfight more appealing than it might otherwise have been.

Still, he was a cop, and trained to defuse volatile situations rather than encourage them. "Do you really think physical's the way to go here, Ty?"

"What I think," his cousin snapped, "is that you've messed with Sadie's head the same way you did with Lisa Johnson's."

"Who's Lisa Johnson?"

"Twelfth grade biology. You dissected a frog together."

"Well, Jesus." But his cousin was dead serious and slammed the heel of his hand into the side of Eli's truck.

"I was engaged to Sadie until you came along."

Brady stepped between them. "Don't you think this is a bit counterproductive? Also, if we're keeping score, I'm the one who took Lisa Johnson to the prom. Spiked the punch, too."

One of Eli's eyebrows winged up. "That was you?"

"It was watered-down vodka—which is neither here nor there. Lisa Johnson's not the point. Sadie is."

"The point," Ty retorted thin-lipped, "is that someone threatened Sadie's life yesterday. Yet here you are, Eli, on the Hollow Road—and where the hell is she? I'll tell you where. She's out at the farm of a man who's a taxidermist and who also has a corn maze big enough to swallow Rhode Island."

Eli controlled his expression and his temper. "You know all that, and yet here you are, as well, accusing me, among other things, of being a crappy cop."

"Sadie's—"

"Got a mind of her own." Despite the assertion, guilt began to slither in his stomach. "She's also not alone. Orley's with her. And Leamer's expecting her."

"I guess that's just one of the many difference between us, cousin. I wouldn't have delegated the responsibility."

"You see Sadie as a responsibility? Not sure she'll appreciate that."

"I'm sure," Brady murmured.

"You're deflecting the blame," Ty ground out.

"No, I'm being reasonable. You're suggesting I should glue myself to her side whether she wants me there or not, to which I repeat, she's got a mind of her own."

"You always have an answer, don't you, a way to twist what you don't want to hear?"

"It's a Blume trait. Sadie's her own woman, Ty, Orley's a former kickboxing champion and Ben Leamer's a staple in the community."

"So, nothing to worry about."

The guilt tangled into slippery knots. Eli kept the curses inside and his features neutral, but dammit, his cousin wasn't wrong. And both the cop in him and the man who'd allowed Sadie to become a fever in his brain had managed to miss it.

"Doing things by the book never suited you, did it?" Ty set his jaw. "You just rewrite it to suit your purpose."

"I don't see how—" Brady began.

"Shut up. I'm talking to Eli—who showed up oh so conveniently on the heels of the first threat Sadie received. How do I know it wasn't you who killed the stupid bird and issued those threats?"

"If you believe I'm deranged, you don't. Not sure how a roll in the mud'll change anything, but I'm game." Holding his hands out to the side, Eli fixed his gaze on his cousin's face. "Go for it."

He knew Ty would have accepted the invitation in a heartbeat if an approaching vehicle hadn't diverted everyone's attention.

"Sadie?" Like a switch flipped in his head, Eli's focus shifted. "What the hell did she do with Orley?"

"She looks pissed," Brady noted. "If she's also got contusions, I'd say you probably shouldn't have left them alone together."

Eli heard him, but he'd already covered half the distance to the Land Rover. When she shoved the door open and hopped out, she did look angry. But what made his blood run cold was that she looked even more agitated.

He caught her arms before she took two steps. And only vaguely questioned the wisdom of doing so when her eyes flashed a warning.

"I need to move," she said through her teeth. "Nothing

personal, Eli, but if I don't walk this off, I'm liable to kick something. Or someone."

He studied her face for a moment, then stepped back, hands raised. "Talk to me," he told her. "Straight, no side trips, or I'm liable to go all cop on you."

A half smile appeared. "You'll do that anyway." She sent the black clouds a smoldering look. "I said—stop raining! Here." She shoved a white envelope at him. "My sick wall writer left this for me in Ben Leamer's corn maze. And I say 'left,' but I really mean 'planted.' He was in the maze with me, Eli. With us. With Orley and me. Orley stayed at the Leamer Farm because the guy who gave me the card also drugged old Ben. Between Orley and me and his hired hand, we managed to get two cups of coffee into Ben's system. He's fuzzy but otherwise okay."

Calling himself every foul name he could think of, Eli handed the card to Ty and concentrated on Sadie. "How do you know the guy was in the maze?"

A tremor rippled through her. "He phoned me. He said he'd hoped I'd go in. He attached the envelope to an effigy of Hezekiah Blume as a raven."

Ty scowled. "Did you or Orley see anything suspicious?"

"Only the ghosts our minds invented." Calmer now, Sadie breathed out. "I think we panicked a little."

Eli cycled through the possibilities. "Are you sure the caller was actually in the maze when he contacted you, though?"

"I'm…not sure, no." Her anger faded as her curiosity grew. "Is that significant?"

"Hardly." Ty examined the card from several angles.

"Possibly," Eli said.

"Why?" Brady offered an apologetic shrug. "Sorry, Eli, but if I'm following this, I have to wonder why it would matter whether or not some guy who gave Sadie a strange card and an equally strange phone call was watching her while they talked."

Eli saw Sadie's eyes flick from him to Ty and back. Yeah, she felt it, he thought, the charge in the air that was more electric than last night's storm.

"It's a detail," he said. "Maybe important, maybe not, but a piece of the puzzle one way or the other."

Watchful herself now, Sadie motioned at the squad car. "Ty, your two-way just went off."

"What?" He surfaced as if from a deep fog.

"Two-way?" She pointed. "Someone needs you."

"Right." He blinked. "Right. Damn. Okay, my jurisdiction here, people. Card stays with me while I deal with whatever problem's on the other end of my radio. Much as I hate to say it, Eli, you and Brady need to head out to the Leamer Farm. Sadie?"

She retracted her finger. "Sorry, but I need to go back to Ben's place."

"Right," he said again.

"I've covered stories like this before, Ty. The solution's always in the details." Walking over, she placed her hands on his shoulders and kissed his cheek. "If Eli's right, what's happening to me goes back twenty years to my cousin Laura's death.

"And if he's wrong?"

She stepped back, as much from the envelope as her former fiancé, Eli suspected.

"A monster's a monster. If that's what we're dealing with, it might be a good idea to remember that nothing and no one sleeps forever."

BEN LEAMER WAS still groggy when they reached the farm. The doctor hadn't arrived yet, but with the infusion of a little fear of God from a still-rattled Orley, he was happy enough to let Brady examine him.

While Brady obliged, Sadie led Eli through the corn maze. Hezekiah, minus envelope, put in an encore appearance. Eli noted the time of the call she'd received, asked her and Orley a thousand questions and was doing something on his iPhone when Brady emerged from the house.

"Regular doctor should give Ben a once-over, but he's a tough old guy. He was chloroformed. You'd have smelled it right off," he said to Eli. "Orley didn't, but then she was pretty freaked, and, bottom line, there's no real reason for her or Sadie to have recognized it."

Pressing on the tension knots in her neck, Sadie wandered around the farmyard. "All I smelled was his sister-in-law's sauerkraut."

"Why didn't you call Eli from the house?" Brady asked her.

"I tried, but Ben's line is down."

"And the bog's a notorious dead zone for cell phones." Eli leaned against the Land Rover. "Two-ways work, but that's it."

"Be glad anything works on the Hollow Road." Shouldering his instrument bag, Brady glanced at Orley, who was marching toward them, grim faced and hugging her arms across her chest. "Hard to believe it's only eleven o'clock. That being said, I have three pointy teeth to extract and a batch of anesthetic to pick up. Take care, Sadie. Watch for stray uppercuts, Eli."

"I am not doing favors for anyone ever again," Orley muttered in passing. "Later, people."

Sadie willed the stabbing pain in her skull down to a manageable level before dropping her hands. "At the risk of sounding like a whiny child, Eli, why are we still here? Shouldn't you and Ty be punching each other out or something?"

He gave the screen of his iPhone a final tap and looked up. "I should have come here with you."

The beginnings of a smile touched her lips. "Did Ty say that?"

"Yeah, but the thought had already occurred."

"In that case, Lieutenant, listen up and pass this on. I am not a maiden in distress, and I don't want or need you or Ty or even Orley dogging me everywhere I go."

"Sadie, Laura—"

"Didn't realize her life was in danger. At best, she was probably thinking pest. Believe me, I'm thinking something very different."

Pushing off from the Land Rover, Eli advanced on her. "Did you tell that to the guy who called you in the maze?"

"No, but I didn't go, 'Eek,' and faint, either. I took a self-defense course while I was in D.C. Don't," she warned, and drilled a finger into his chest when his advance brought him to within a foot of where she stood. "I'm not in the mood to fend off all the sexual vibes that bombard me whenever I make the mistake of touching you. I have work to do at the *Chronicle*. Stuff to approve, printing presses to swear at...."

"I get the picture, Sadie. I also still owe Rooney a canine favor."

His eyes glinted just enough to have hers narrowing in suspicion. "Why are you being so agreeable all of a sudden?"

"Maybe I'm just giving you credit for being able to handle yourself in any situation."

And maybe Rooney would breeze through another full century of life, but Sadie doubted it.

Keeping her finger on his chest, she nudged him back a

step. "Let's do it this way. You can follow me to the Hollow in your truck. We part company and maybe, maybe," she emphasized, "meet up again at Rooney's favorite dockside haunt around dinnertime."

"It's one plan," Eli acknowledged. "But if you're up for it, I have an alternative."

"Does it involve you playing watchdog as part of some clever plot to circumvent me?"

"No, it involves you and me making what will undoubtedly be a messy trip into the north woods."

Her laugh was mostly disbelief. "You want to visit my great-grandfather? Now? In the middle of hell week?"

"I was thinking more along the lines of us having a chat with Cal Kilgore."

"Ah, right. Laura's former boyfriend." Her gaze traveled northward. "Directions to the cabin would be an easy get. Not sure how happy he'll be to see us. Howard Hughes was a party animal compared to Cal after Laura died." Mistrust crept back in. "At the risk of sounding contrary, why do you want me to go with you? Or is this part of that clever plot I mentioned before?"

In spite of the finger still pushing into his chest, Eli caught and raised her chin. "What this is, Sadie, is me being impressed."

"By what?"

"You. Back on the Hollow Road, you told the rain to stop falling." A smile appeared as he kissed the tip of her nose. "A few seconds later, it did."

Chapter Ten

"I hope you realize, even my formidable strength of will won't hold the rain back indefinitely."

"Just do your best for as long as you can, and I'm good."

No, he wasn't, Sadie thought with a flicker of amusement. But then she wouldn't be, either, if it was her vehicle taking a beating instead of his.

There'd been details to deal with before they headed north. First and foremost, she'd wanted to check on her cleaning man, Bobby. He'd lost his cell phone but was otherwise unharmed. Next, she'd contacted Molly and asked her to feed Cocoa in the event that she and Eli didn't make it home as planned. She'd attempted to call her great-grandfather on his SAT phone, but the thickening cloud cover made satellite communication impossible. Last, because she'd ventured into the north woods enough times to know, she'd loaded a canvas pack with personal items and emergency supplies, and stowed it in Eli's truck.

From the passenger seat, she watched a line of ever-greens, as tall as the towers of Bellam Manor, sway like happy drunks.

"If memory serves," she mused, "Cal gave me the willies when I was a kid. His eyes moved independently of each other, causing many of the Hollow residents to avoid him like the plague. It goes without saying that everyone who knew Laura seriously questioned her taste in males."

Eli braked at an odd-shaped fork. "Go for it."

She ticked a considering finger. "Left."

"Are you sure?"

"Eli, of the two of us in this truck, who's holding back the rain?"

Lips twitching, he took the left fork. "Tell me, how strongly does Molly believe in your witchy heritage?"

"Hard to say. She's superstitious on one hand and completely practical on the other."

"She told me Bellam Manor wouldn't turn on one of its own."

"That's a relief. Now if we could get it to tell us who broke in last night, we'd be set." She let a few seconds pass before sliding her gaze sideways. "Eli, what's the deal with you and Ty?"

"No deal, other than if I'm smart, I won't walk in front of him after sunset."

"There's a cheerful prospect."

"Guy's in love with you, Sadie."

She smiled a little. "He's really not, you know. He might still love me, but not the way you're interpreting it."

"He wanted to trade punches on the Hollow Road."

"What he wanted was to show you that he's as good a cop as you are."

"Ty knows he's a good cop. As much as it pains me to say this, he'd have been a decent husband, too."

Now her smile blossomed. "Every part of you just clenched up. But you can relax. Bellam females, from Nola to now, have had a notorious lack of success where relationships are concerned. Ask either of my parents which one of them screwed their marriage up worse, and they'll both tell you it was my mother." Leaning forward, she regarded the bruised sky. "Aw, see what you've done? It's starting to rain again. You rattled my concentration with that 'decent husband' remark. Now my mind's stuck in the bedroom."

"Pretty sure we were talking about you and Ty, Sadie."

"Yes, but I'm in your truck, post-Boston, and I have all these sexual vibes jittering around inside me."

His lips curved, but the gleam in his eyes smacked of danger. "Is that how you see us? As opposing masses of barely controlled vibes?"

"I used the word *jitter,* Eli, specifically because jitters are in fact controllable. By women, anyway."

"Is that your opinion of all men, or just me?"

"Oh, I have a much higher opinion of you than I do of most men." Her smile teased him now. "You charmed me in Boston, Eli. The bigger miracle is that you also charmed my aunt, who's as practical as Molly and wouldn't know a jitter if it bit her. She thought you were hot, and I was insane not to jump you."

"Yeah, well, that same aunt told me that you were her favorite niece, and if I so much as made you frown, she'd turn me into a jackass."

Sadie waved off the remark. "She uses that threat on men all the time. It's a private joke. In her opinion, there isn't a male alive who needs a hit of magic to become a jackass. It's a natural condition."

He grinned. "I could refute that, or shut up and drive. I'll go with the easier option."

"Making you the smartest jackass in the class. Turn right," she said without looking. "Follow the so-called road as far as you can, and I'll do what *I* can, sans spell book, to keep the ground underneath us as navigable as possible."

"Appreciate that, sweetheart. While you're at it—" he

nodded through the windshield "—you might want to tell that moose thirty feet in front of us to move along."

HE'D EXPECTED HER to jolt. Instead, the smile that lit every one of her features had his brain blurring with lust.

"She's gorgeous." Clearly captivated, Sadie scooted forward in her seat. "The size of them never fails to amaze me. This one's bigger than most males."

Noting a movement, Eli gestured. "This one has a calf."

"Really? Where? Oh, it's gorgeous, too."

He reached into his waistband. "Don't know about baby, but Mama moose is a hell of a lot more than gorgeous."

"The word you're looking for is dangerous. But only if she sees us as a threat." She made an uncertain motion. "Then again, it's mating season, so that could be a problem if there's a horny male in the vicinity. Present company excluded."

"Funny." But when he started to open the door, she caught his arm.

"Eli, you are not going to shoot that magnificent creature."

He half smiled. "I thought we agreed I wasn't the biggest jackass on the planet. I only want to move mother and child along before a hormonal bull shows up and sees my truck as a worthy opponent."

"What makes you think…? Oh, never mind. Just do it."

Four harmless shots later, Mama moose, having carefully considered her options, nudged her calf along and clomped into the woods behind it.

"Huh." Sadie sat back. "Bear would have been more fun."

"Proof that you've never ventured into the high Rockies. No encounter with a grizzly could ever be called fun."

She waited until he slammed the door, then reaching

over the console, grabbed a handful of his hair and yanked his mouth onto hers. When she drew away, her gray eyes glittered. "I love a man who can transition from back alleys to the backwoods without missing a beat."

He'd figure out what she'd said, Eli reflected, when the flames at the back of his throat subsided and his heart—which had missed several beats—kick-started again.

A blast of wet wind bore down on the truck. Releasing his hair, Sadie dropped back into her seat. "Looks like my focus is shot, Lieutenant. Good thing we brought our rain gear."

Rain gear, right. Eli struggled to think past the need currently blasting through his bloodstream. The road they were on ended two miles from Kilgore's cabin—as the raven flew.

Given that Sadie had long since mastered the art of a guileless expression, he could only speculate as to what was running through her mind right now. Probably nothing his male pride wanted to hear. Happy enough to let it ride, he flicked on the wipers and upped the volume of Whitesnake on his iPod.

By the time they ran out of drivable track, the shadows between the trees made gloomy afternoon feel like weird twilight.

"Rooney says the north woods are even more haunted than the hollow." Sadie zipped herself into a bright yellow raincoat. "I'm curious to know what that means."

"It means he's got a friend with a still in the area."

She pulled on a pair of rubber boots. "Eli, Rooney doesn't need to come all the way out here for his whiskey. Ben Leamer—" she caught his level look and ramped up her smile "—has a refreshment stand in one of his barns. Kids get a free bottle of fruit juice with the price of admission."

"Uh-huh. Does Ty know about this stand?"

"No need." She scooped her hair into a ponytail, popped a ball cap on her head and pulled up her hood. "He doesn't have any kids. Ready?"

He'd leave it alone, Eli decided. Rooney had survived without his help for more than a century. If they didn't stop the person threatening her, Sadie might not make next Friday.

Over his dead body, of course, but his darker sense didn't think that would be much of an issue in her stalker's mind.

Rain continued to fall in miserable wind-driven sheets. When the ground gave way and almost sent Sadie into a rocky chasm, Eli barely managed to catch her.

Rebalanced, she exhaled. "Imagine how bad this would be if my mind wasn't holding back the worst of it."

"Given the strength of those gusts, we'd probably be landing in Oz about now. Keep to the right," Eli told her. "The path's higher there."

Not that it made much difference since calling the ground a quagmire would have been a generous description.

"We should have hired a helicopter to drop us onto Cal's roof." Sadie began the tricky descent into a wide gully. "Between last night's storm and this one, if he's home and dry, I say Laura's ex isn't the person who threatened me."

But still worth the trip in Eli's estimation. As far as he could tell from the information on file, both Cal Kilgore's mother and his grandmother had alibied him for the night of Laura's murder. Although similar, their stories hadn't quite jibed in terms of where he'd been on the property and what they'd believed he was doing.

The points were small, but interesting when added to the fact that Cal had personally delivered three shipments of hardware to Bangor this fall. In other words, a guy who seldom surfaced had passed through Raven's Hollow as many times in one month as Brady had seen him in the last fifteen years.

"Do you remember what Kilgore looked like?" he asked Sadie from behind.

She shoved through a tangle of branches. "I remember him as tall, with long, stringy brown hair that he wore in a ponytail."

"What about his features?"

"Sorry, all fuzzy. Guess the guy didn't do it for me when I was seven. The story I heard is that Cal's mother left the Hollow when she was found to be in possession of a stolen cameo pendant. She used to clean houses part-time. She claimed she accidently dusted the cameo into the pocket of her apron. The owner didn't press charges, and a few weeks later, Mrs. K just sort of faded from sight."

"What about Grandma K?"

"Molly said she died in her sleep while watching the Shopping Channel."

"Wouldn't anyone?"

Sadie hopped over a deep crevice. "Molly also said that Grandma Kilgore and Rooney used to share a corner table at Two Toes Joe's Bar on Saturday nights."

An image he did not want to see slid through Eli's head. "Okay, you need to stop right there."

"Sundays at Joe's were reserved for Rooney and Ben Leamer's sister."

"Any time you wanna stop."

"Rooney and Ben's sister used to hold hands between drinks. Oh, and there was also—"

"Sadie." Snagging her collar, Eli brought her to a smooth halt. "Shut up." To make sure she did, he tipped her head back and set his mouth on hers.

Bad idea, he realized instantly. The taste of her simply blanked his mind. Fortunately, it also set off about a thousand warning bells. With the last of them clanging loudly, he reeled in an urge to take her on the forest floor, and while he could still form a rational thought, he murmured a quiet "Got to stop doing that."

He nudged her ahead of him on the path, where they carried on in silence for several minutes. He figured she was channeling her mental energy upward rather than cursing him, because with every step they took, the wind gusts grew more fitful and the rain slowed from a downpour to a steady drizzle. He sensed he should be grateful.

"You're welcome," she called over her shoulder. Boosting herself onto a fallen tree, she swung her legs over and hopped onto a weedy slope. "Cal's cabin's dead ahead. I don't see any chimney smoke, but there might be a light—"

It was as far as she got. Metal glinted in one of the windows. Eli heard the sound of glass breaking and glimpsed a long barrel through the scrub. He shoved Sadie to the ground a split second before a hailstorm of bullets erupted.

SADIE COULDN'T SEE or think or feel. She could only breathe in shallow gasps. It was better than being shot, she supposed, but barely.

The initial barrage of bullets stopped at twelve. Although half of them came from Eli's Police Special, he kept her firmly beneath him during the entire exchange. When the last echo subsided, the weight on her rib cage lifted, allowing her to draw her first desperate breath.

"Are you hit?" Eli yanked her zipper down and pulled her top up. "Talk to me, Sadie. Where's the wound?"

With black spots still swimming, she sucked in more air. "I'm not…" The word *hurt* dissolved when she saw the blood on her raincoat. "Eli, stop. It's not me, it's you. You're the one who was shot."

He frowned, glanced down—then shoved her under him again as five more bullets zinged through the low leaves.

She wriggled out far enough to shout, "Cal, stop shooting. It's Sadie Bellam and Eli Blume. We're not here to—whatever you're thinking. We need to talk to you!"

"Get off my land," a man's voice bellowed back. "I protect what's mine."

"You must have known the guy, Eli." She wriggled out farther. "Say something buddylike. Then roll over so I can look at your shoulder."

"It'll keep." He stilled her busy hands. "You sound friendlier than I do. Identify yourself again, and mention Laura."

She raised her voice. "Cal, I'm Laura's cousin Sadie, from the Hollow."

"I don't care if you're General Lee come back from the dead. I want you and your pal to haul your trespassing butts off my land, or else I'll shoot 'em off."

"O-kay," Eli said in a tone that fell somewhere between enlightenment and anticipation.

"We're trapped, and you're bleeding." Sadie yanked his T-shirt down. "It's just a graze, but there's nothing okay about any of this."

"His accent's wrong."

"I—" she thought for a moment "—didn't notice that," she realized, and replayed the shooter's warning. "Mississippi?"

"Or Louisiana."

"So, not Cal, and not friendly. But in Cal's cabin with a gun."

"Rifle."

"Aimed at our trespassing butts."

"And where's Cal?" Eli wondered aloud. "Alive, dead or somewhere in between?"

"I see two grazes, Eli, one on your shoulder, another on your upper arm."

His eyes remained on the cabin. "They're scratches, Sadie. I've had worse." He shifted his weight. "I need to get down there without him seeing me. Can you keep him talking?"

She could argue, Sadie supposed, or accept and deal as he was apparently doing. Gnashing her teeth, she glanced one last time at his injuries before switching her attention to the cabin. "Not sure how long he'll want to chat."

"Do what you can." Reaching into the top of his boot, he drew a second gun. "You've got fifteen shots. Brace when you squeeze the trigger. This thing has a wicked kick."

"That's so reassuring."

"Have you ever fired a gun before?"

"Only in my dreams at an unpleasant boss. Better for all concerned if talking works."

Pressing a hand to her neck, Eli cautioned her to keep low, then vanished into the underbrush. And people called her a witch?

"We're not here to hurt you," she shouted downward. "We just want to talk to Cal."

A bullet clipped the trunk of an elder behind her and sent bits of bark flying.

"I don't give a damn who, what or why, lady. Ain't no one in this foxhole but me and Old Faithful, and we'd as soon kill you as look at you."

"Like I haven't figured that out," she muttered. Double-handing the gun, she braced her arms on a rock and tried again. "Look, you're in Cal's Kilgore's cabin. How were we supposed to know he'd moved?"

"Well, you know now, so beat it and let me be."

He released three more shots, one of them so close to her cheek she felt the air move as it whizzed past.

Fighting to keep her voice even, she countered, "If we leave, do we have your word you won't shoot us in the back?"

She swore she heard him snicker. "Yeah, sure, you got my word. You want me to give it in your language, too?"

Sadie opened her mouth, closed it again. Her language?

She glimpsed a movement through the foliage. A second later, three rapid-fire shots exploded. Glass shattered, wood splintered and someone—not Eli, she prayed—gave a short, sharp cry.

Her arms ached from holding them over a rock. Lowering her forehead to her wrists, she counted to five, heard nothing except the wind in the trees. She had to believe Eli had made it inside. But had he done so safely?

Raising her head, she started to call out. She actually had Eli's name on her lips when the underbrush rustled behind her. Rolling sideways, she snapped the gun up. But had no time to fire as a large black mass leaped at her.

Chapter Eleven

Eli distracted the shooter by tossing a stone through one of the side windows. He fired as he ran along the porch, then kicked at the latch of a rickety-looking door.

Inside, the man with the rifle spun, ready on the trigger. Anticipating him, Eli used a branch he'd snagged in the woods, knocked the barrel away, then grabbed the tip and yanked.

When the rifle clattered, the shooter stumbled backward, smashing a table and landing on the floor, where he thrashed his arms like an addict in the throes.

A fist plowed into Eli's bad shoulder, but once he had the guy on his stomach, it was over.

"Kill me!" his prisoner ordered. "You kill me now, I don't care how. I ain't gonna rot in one of your stinking prisons."

"Wanna bet?" Holding him down with a knee in the small of his back, and his gun pressed to a grimy nape, Eli batted aside an erratic arm and found a lamp cord. The struggle that followed had him longing for a pair of handcuffs and uniformed backup. However, despite his throbbing shoulder, the guy, who had a good thirty years on him, was trussed and turned inside a minute.

"Kill me," the man demanded while Eli wound a second cord around his feet. "I got a right to die with dignity."

The words registered as much as the ravings of a junkie ever did. It wasn't until his gaze landed on the big, round table near the kitchen that those white-noise ravings gave way to a sharp click.

There were two bowls. Two bowls, two mugs, two plates.

Like a solid blow to the midsection, the truth stripped the air from his lungs and turned everything inside him to ice.

The shooter wasn't alone.

Cursing his lack of forethought, Eli grabbed his gun and, shoving in a fresh ammo clip, ran back to where he'd left Sadie.

THE BLACK MASS would have landed on her if the ground hadn't been sloped and relatively free of obstructions. Sadie reacted quickly, but he still managed to pin her hips.

She heard snarls like those of an enraged bull. That he wasn't actually a bull only made its way into a side pocket of her brain. The rest was more concerned with gaining her freedom and, barring that, figuring out how to shoot him before he tore her apart.

With Eli's gun still tightly clutched, she used her other hand to scoop up a handful of mud and pebbles and fling it in his eyes—wherever they were.

A floppy hood covered his head and obscured his features. Her mind immediately conjured Ezekiel's face, but that was her nightmare. The man on top of her wasn't Ezekiel Blume, and waking up wouldn't save her from whatever horror was in his mind.

When he stretched out for the gun, she managed to buck him sideways and get an elbow up into his jaw. The impact knocked him back far enough for her to free a foot. Unable to kick him in the crotch, she brought her heel down on his calf and at the same time sank her teeth into his wrist.

Swearing, he snatched his arm away and squared up for a punch. His knuckles clipped her cheekbone, but when he groped for the gun again, she worked her knee loose and shoved it between his legs.

That he didn't crumple had ripples of fresh fear racing along her nerve ends. She didn't know if she tasted blood or only imagined it. Whatever the case, the gun remained in her possession, and that was key.

She used her heel again, but this time he slammed a forearm across her windpipe and pressed until her vision went spotty. She was endeavoring to bite his hand when suddenly his weight and the spots were gone, and she was skidding downhill.

"What the…?" Startled, with her lungs screaming for air, she dug in and scrambled to her knees. By the time she whipped the gun into position, however, all she saw was her captor and Eli disappearing into the underbrush below.

Pushing the hair from her face, Sadie tracked their movements. It was easy enough to do. Fists slammed repeatedly into bone and flesh, and the growls were growing feral.

She could help, she thought, and found a rock. Curling her fingers around it, she slid awkwardly down the slope.

Maybe Eli could take the guy—probably could, in fact—but his opponent was big, strong and likely hadn't been grazed by two bullets. So…

Using her senses, she pushed through the bushes. When she spotted them, she didn't aim—no time for that— merely trusted her instincts and brought the rock down hard on the man's neck. A second later, Eli kicked him up against a tree. Sadie saw part of a beard, heard a whoosh of breath and watched the man slide bonelessly into the mud.

Regaining his feet, Eli took a single unsteady step. He wiped at a trickle of blood on his mouth as he angled his gun down. "Twitch a muscle, and you'll be leaving these woods in a box. Did he hurt you?" he asked Sadie in the same breath.

"No more than I hurt him." Curious, she eased forward and gave the black hood a tug.

Stringy gray-brown hair, no longer confined, lay in rats' tails across a pair of sallow cheeks. His eyes remained shut while his mouth opened and closed like a woozy codfish's.

She straightened with a sigh. "Cal Kilgore, two decades later. Now I remember the face."

"Who are you?" he slurred from the ground. "And what're you doing on my land?"

She would have answered, but it seemed he wasn't as woozy as he looked. A leg snaked out in Eli's direction.

"I've met smarter," she murmured, and wisely backed off.

A few seconds later, with Cal spread-eagled in a mound of lichens, his eyes wheeling from a punch to the face, she smiled at Eli, who stood shaking out a fist. "Impressive, Lieutenant. However, if you and Laura's former stud are done here, we should probably think about heading down to the cabin. It's getting awfully close to dinnertime."

Stashing his gun, Eli bent to one knee and hauled his prisoner to a sitting position. "I've been inside that cabin, sweetheart. Pretty sure you won't want to eat there."

"That wasn't quite what I meant." She helped him lever Cal to his feet. "Unless I'm hallucinating, that black thing heading down the hill from the trees is a very large, probably very hungry bear."

"YOU'RE WAY OUT of your jurisdiction, Eli," Cal accused thirty minutes later. "You also didn't identify yourself as a cop. Not to me or to my uncle. You press charges, we'll press charges."

"Then I'll press charges," Sadie added. "And we'll turn the courtroom into a three-ring circus."

She spoke from the far side of the room where she sat cross-legged on the floor, observing Cal's uncle while he snored, jerked and shuddered in his—she supposed you could call it sleep. Judging from the empty prescription bottle on the kitchen counter, he'd taken more than a few tranquilizers that afternoon.

She indicated the older man's military tattoos. "Post-traumatic stress syndrome?"

"Used to be called shell shock." Cal fixed his left eye on her. "He spent four years in Nam and every year after that paying for the pleasure." His other eye glared at Eli. "You've got no business showing up here unannounced."

"We announced ourselves loud and clear to your uncle." Eli flexed the shoulder Sadie had done her best to clean and bandage. "His response was to open fire on us."

"Shell shock," Cal repeated.

Sadie regarded the grizzled man who looked like a hermit and snored like a buzz saw. "He needs more help than you can give him, Cal."

"Don't we all, Sadie Bellam? Me, I could use a double shot of the whiskey my uncle polished off two days ago, but life's always been a kick in the crotch that way. Oh, no, wait. That was you who kicked me."

"After you jumped me," she reminded. "Come on, Cal, you and Eli are distantly related. Help us out just a bit here."

"Why should I?"

Eli stared him down. "Because odds are that whiskey your uncle polished off came from a storehouse I noticed that's sitting on your land. And helping us is a good start toward helping me forget that once we're back in the Hollow."

Cal started to boil up, but reconsidered when he looked

at his sleeping uncle. "Aw, hell, go on, then, fire away, Sadie."

"Were you upset when Laura ended your relationship?"

"Not upset enough to do her."

"You didn't come to the funeral."

He showed his teeth in a nonsmile. "Ex-boyfriend. Think that one's been established."

"It has, yes. A month after Laura was buried, someone left a bouquet of wildflowers on her grave."

"Good for someone."

"On the anniversary of your first date with her." She sent Eli a blithe smile. "I went into the *Chronicle*'s archives on my computer last night after the break-in at the manor and found an article. One of the reporters interviewed your grandmother, Cal. And please don't tell me the flowers were a coincidence, because somebody's doing to me what he did to Laura, and it's freaking me out."

"It's pissing me off." Moving to an unbroken window, Eli made a thorough scan of the clearing.

"If you're looking for Mr. Bear, Eli, he only comes around when the urge strikes. I let him raid my trash cans, he lets me pass when we accidentally bump. I gave the police everything I had way back when, Sadie. Nothing more I can tell you now."

But she sensed from the way neither of his eyes met hers that there was in fact something more. Something he hadn't told the police, or possibly anyone.

She studied his body language. Irritable with traces of resentment around the edges.

"If it makes a difference, Cal, I don't think you're involved in Laura's death or in any of the threats I've received."

"Haven't heard the lieutenant say that yet."

"Storehouse," Eli reminded him from the window.

Cal paced in stiff strides around the room. "I saw my

life going differently back then. Figured Laura and me'd
get married, but I guess the bad-boy thing wore thin. I
said some stuff after she broke it off. Not that I wanted
to kill her, but that I thought maybe she was seeing another guy. She said she wasn't and wouldn't be for a long
time, because she was going off to college, then down to
Ecuador. She wanted to be a nurse and work where there
was a need."

"Was that the last time you talked to her?" Sadie asked.

"Last time I called her, yeah. I went into a funk for a
few weeks afterward. Didn't work or wash, just watched
TV and drank beer." One eye rolled, the other remained
on her face. "She phoned me two nights before she died,
mad as a hornet. She wanted to know if I had put a big,
folded piece of paper in her gym bag, because what was
on it was sick and low, and it wasn't going to change anything between us."

Sadie's stomach muscles tightened. "Do you know what
the paper said?"

"All she told me was that it was sick and like something
she figured I might do if I was drunk and feeling ornery.
Fact is, I *was* drunk, but truth is, I didn't know what the
hell she was talking about. That's when she got all pissy
and said I might as well have signed my name to it."

Sadie ran the thought through her head. "That's—really interesting, actually."

"Not to mention incriminating," Eli put in. "Keep talking, Cal. What did you say back to her?"

A shoulder jerked. "Stuff she didn't like, nothing that
came out like a threat. It wasn't until right before she
slammed the phone down that she finally told me what
she meant." He raised and wiggled all ten fingers. "I'm
what you call ambidextrous. Means I can write with either hand. But the writing looks different, depending on

what hand I use. That's why she thought I'd given her the paper. Because partway through the message, the writing changed. Those were the last words she spoke to me, and every one came out clear as a bell. She said, 'The writing changed.'"

LATE AFTERNOON BLED far too quickly into early evening. They had to leave because no way did Sadie want to be on foot in the north woods after dark. Lions and tigers and bears, she could handle, but not a crazed killer who shot ravens and, twenty years after the fact, saw her as his next victim.

They made it to Eli's truck less than ten minutes before the last shimmer of daylight faded to black.

While the headlights provided a measure of comfort, they also turned the drizzle into thin white needles and revealed vague movements that gave the shadows life and fed the fearful chill that had been making Sadie's teeth want to chatter since Cal had talked about his final conversation with her cousin.

Not for the first time, she wished she could push her fingers directly into her brain. Anything to blot out the monstrous images that played and replayed like a carousel of horror.

"I've got this Jekyll and Hyde film clip running through my head," she confessed as they drove. "Except in my case, Jekyll's as dangerous as Hyde. And just as mad. Apparently."

A smile ghosted around Eli's lips. "With Ezekiel Blume in the starring dual role?"

"It would have to be Ezekiel, wouldn't it? He wanted his brother's wife dead. It turned out Nola was able to cheat death, but initially, everyone involved believed she'd gone to hell where she belonged. Laura wasn't a witch, though, Eli, and all teasing aside, neither am I."

"I don't think this is a witch-hunt, Sadie."

"What, then? Obsession?"

"Mine forever," he repeated.

She sighed. "I guess in a weird sort of way, death could be construed as forever. Someone wanted Laura. Couldn't have her. Killed her. It's straightforward enough from a psychological standpoint in that obsessed people frequently turn on the person after whom they lust. But when you factor in what Cal told us about the writing changing, straightforward becomes a wobbly line to nowhere."

"Unless Cal's the murderer and, as Laura believed, he simply changed hands while writing a message that only she saw."

"Obsessed with Laura, I get. Obsessed with me, not at all. Except for our red hair, Laura and I look—looked— nothing alike. Also, the last time Cal and I met face-to-face before today, I was a kid. I really think you can scratch him from the suspect list."

"Move him farther down anyway. Another possibility is that we're dealing with a split personality. It would account for the fact that the writing changed and obsession ultimately descended into death. Not to mention this morning's reference to an inner monster."

Sadie swore her brain was going to explode. "That's not much of a comfort, is it? Go left at the next fork. The road improves, and my great-grandfather's place is only a mile farther on."

Eli glanced at her, then gave her hair a light tug. "Ninety-nine years old, huh? And living alone in the middle of haunted nowhere."

His deliberately humorous tone eased a portion of her tension. "I know what you're thinking. Major neglect on our part. But there's a twelve-member family who make canoes and live in a collection of cabins half a mile west of Great-grandfather's place. One or another of them checks on him faithfully morning, noon and night. He wasn't happy in the Hollow, Eli. He's very happy here." She smiled. "He also loves to play chess."

"How do you know I...ah, right. Rooney."

"Man's a font." She relaxed more as the road leveled off. "I only wish he was clairvoyant. Or I was."

"Are you completely convinced that Molly isn't?"

"Yes, but you can decide for yourself. Before we left the Hollow today, she told me not to make any plans for Monday night."

"Do I want to know why?"

"Probably not. She's arranging a séance."

Chapter Twelve

"You played a game of chess with that old buzzard?"

An outraged Rooney brought his cane down on the front desk of the Raven's Hollow Police Station and made the deputy jump. Eli merely raised an eyebrow.

"That old buzzard beat the crap out of me in under three hours without a drop of alcohol in his system."

"Probably smokes funny cigarettes instead." Rapping his cane on the floor now, Rooney raised his voice. "Where's the damn dog, Ty? My former grandson here says he's a winner. He's gonna get Brady to give him a once-over. Then he's going to fetch Sadie from the *Chronicle*. I want her down at Joe's bar to cover the fights."

Ty came in with a brown and white bulldog on a leash. "I hope we're talking televised fights."

"Nope, live action. Cove versus Hollow. And no, I'm not naming names, because you always take it upon your chiefly self to lecture the participants until their morale is lower than Chopper's jowls." Rooney pushed the leash into Eli's hands. "Take the dog to Brady, stranger, while I remind your spoilsport cousin who in this room is sixty-seven years older than whom."

"Sixty-five." Ty grimaced. "I wasn't a model grade school student."

The old man cackled. "I thought the pair of you would

be forty before you graduated." When Eli's eyes narrowed, he waved his cane. "I meant Ty and Brady. You just trot Chopper over to the v-e-t for that exam while I lay a little guilt trip on your cousin."

"It's Sunday," Eli reminded him. "Brady's day o-f-f."

"Then go up to his apartment and n-a-g him into doing an old man a favor."

More than done with the spelling bee, Eli headed for the door. He turned up his collar against a whippy north wind and jogged with the bulldog down Main Street to the edge of the square.

Bad weather notwithstanding, it was good to be outdoors. He'd spent the better part of the day on his computer, studying Sadie's Facebook and Twitter pages and poring over all the files he could access about the investigation into Laura's death. He'd talked to several people at the *Chronicle* and others who'd known both Laura and Sadie since they were children. Although he'd come up empty in the clue department, he'd enjoyed looking at the vacation pictures Sadie had posted online.

It surprised him to see Orley through the clinic window, counting bags of dog food. Farther in, Brady tapped away on his laptop.

"No more favors," Orley warned when the door swung shut behind him.

"This one's on Brady." Eli unzipped his jacket. "Why's it so hot in here?"

"Molly brought Solomon in an hour ago. Emergency ingrown claw. The dog freaked, we sedated, then had to up the temperature to the high side of unbearable because Molly and Solomon want what they want and Molly doesn't go away until they get it. I woke up with a screaming headache, and listening to Cousin McStrange bitch wasn't something I wanted to add to an already poopy

Sunday. We're doing inventory," she said heavily, and made another tick with her marker. "A little help would be nice."

"Sorry. I'm picking Sadie up at the *Chronicle* after Brady checks out Chopper. She's determined to talk to Ben Leamer, and I gather Ben's equally determined to talk to her."

"Meaning you're gonna tag."

"You got it."

Brady came out, took the leash. "We'll make this quick, in that case. Exam would go faster if you'd take Chopper's temperature for me."

"What, did hell freeze over and no one told me?"

"Coward." Orley snickered over her shoulder. Then she made a sound of disgust as she stared out the window. "Seriously? Break bottles on your own sidewalk, Molly, not ours."

"Perfect." Brady appealed to his cousin. "If you won't help with the dog, at least keep Orley from scratching Molly's eyes out for whatever disaster just occurred."

He'd do it, Eli reflected, if only to escape the cloying heat.

Outside, Orley scowled at the sidewalk. "I am not getting down on my hands and knees to clean up a mess you made because you decided to wobble around on six-inch heels so Ty would notice your legs."

Molly shrank into herself. "It's only ink. It can be eradicated."

"Oh, now, there's a word. What do you think, Eli? Can indelible ink be eradicated?"

He didn't know or care. And he didn't listen to the rest of the barbed exchange. What he did do was look at Molly's unrevealing face. Then down at the bright red ink that seeped like blood across the sidewalk.

"GIVE ME FORTY minutes, Ben." Sadie glanced at the clock on the typesetter's desk. "Maybe an hour. We'll get it done today, I promise. I'm glad you're feeling better." Disconnecting, she raised her voice to her assistant. "Make sure those photos of Rooney's first wedding don't blur when they're enlarged. And don't remove the red from the eyes of the background ravens. It's a cool effect."

"Done and done. You sure you don't mind if I leave early?"

"If I did, you'd feel the negative ions."

"Like I did the time I failed to notice that the camera shop's 'Shot in the Dark' ad layout ran with an *i* in place of the *o?*"

"Exactly like that. I'm off tomorrow, so bright and early, okay?"

"No problem."

The door creaked open and closed, leaving Sadie alone with the cleaning crew and a welter of troubled thoughts.

She knew it was her own fault that she felt unsettled. While Eli and her great-grandfather had played chess last night, she'd foolishly gone over one of the many accounts he'd collected detailing their family's sordid history.

She'd skipped the chapters that dealt with their persecution in Europe and zeroed in on Nola Bellam's life in New England.

An unwed eighteenth century mother, Nola had never named the father of her daughter. Some speculated it was Hezekiah, and that the two of them had had sex after a Halloween-style party at Blume House without Hezekiah ever knowing the name of the young woman he'd bedded. Others claimed the child was Ezekiel's, and he'd known exactly who Nola was.

Sadie didn't buy either story. Her feeling was that Nola had simply fallen under the spell of a handsome stranger who'd been passing through the Hollow en route to parts unknown, and she'd wound up pregnant as a result.

Whatever the case, Nola had come to Hezekiah with a seven-year-old child.

Sadie had fallen asleep with the book in her hands while her great-grandfather and Eli continued their chess match. Of course the dream had snuck in and played out as usual. Until the end.

In this new, altered version, the cloaked shape that appeared after Ezekiel's death missed the mark with its enormous knife. There was no pain in Sadie's chest, no cry of triumph from inside the voluminous hood, and for the first time in memory, she hadn't woken up gasping on the bedroom floor.

In her still-sleeping mind, astonishment had quickly given way to hope.

She'd unpinned her cloak and, twirling it outward, trapped the figure's knife and arm with the hem. The figure had fought to free itself. As it did, the wind swirled up, filling the huge hood with air.

Though she'd never been able to in the past, this time she'd glimpsed a man's face within the folds. Hezekiah's perhaps, or Ezekiel's. The features had been unclear, as if they'd been distorting before her eyes. Or maybe they'd been transforming. Into what or who, she couldn't say.

As suddenly as it had swirled up, the wind died, the hood deflated and only darkness and death remained.

Alone in the silent woods, Sadie had heard the voice again. As the moonlight faded away, it had seemed to whisper directly into her ear.

"You are no longer mine alone, Sadie Bellam. The monster is awake...."

"YOU SHOULD HAVE told me about your dream, Sadie." Still parked in Ben Leamer's farmyard, Eli stowed her camera bag. "Yes, I'm a cop, but I'm also a Blume. I was raised on similar stories. With Rooney, legend trumps history every time."

"For me, legend crowned dream. Or maybe it was the other way around." Mission finally accomplished in terms of Ben's corn maze, Sadie leaned against the side of Eli's truck while he opened the passenger door. "In any case, I had a much better second dream."

Setting his hands on her waist, Eli boosted her onto the truck's running board. "Any reason you didn't mention that before now?"

"I thought about it." She leaned into him. "The thing is, my great-grandfather's not as sexually liberated as yours. Having been at the wrong end of a shotgun wedding himself, he'd have no qualms about threatening you with the same fate in the not-unlikely event that our jittering vibes, in combination with my überhot dream, had gotten the better of our personal resolves and sent us stumbling out to the backseat of your truck."

"Your great-grandfather had a shotgun wedding?"

Laughing, she pushed an elbow into his ribs. "That wasn't the point, Eli."

"I got the point, Sadie. Hot dreams plus hot vibes create explosive situations."

"Then again…" Seated now, she bent forward to brush her lips over his cheek. "As a cop, you'd be accustomed to excessive heat."

"Then again."

Her eyes sparkled as she slid a finger over his jaw. "Is that your subtle way of suggesting we abandon our personal resolves and fumble around in the backseat before we head over to Joe's bar? Because, I promise you, one swig of his green beer, and hot sex will be the last thing on your mind."

He kissed her fingers before closing the door between them. "Is that why Ty doesn't drink?"

"No, he doesn't drink because he likes to be in control of his faculties at all times. He's quite particular about that."

With a look at the darkening sky, Eli climbed into the truck. "Tell me, Sadie, how did it happen that you very nearly married a fussy old lady?"

"He's not..." she began, then remembered that Eli and Ty were cousins and gave his leg a gentle swat. "Ty's a good man, and I wanted, or thought I wanted, Andy Griffith. You know—Mayberry, the fishing hole, Sunday dinners, that kind of thing."

"You wanted to marry Andy of Mayberry?"

"No, I wanted the front porch swing—and you're laughing at me." Her next swat wasn't quite so gentle. "I'm baring my soul here, Eli. Haven't you ever wanted normal?"

His lips twitched. "Okay, first of all, no TV family was ever normal. Second, you don't strike me as a porch swing kind of woman. And third, where you're seeing white picket fences in Mayberry, I'm seeing you waking up one morning and suddenly realizing you're in Stepford."

She sent him an exasperated look. "When I said Ty liked to be in control, I didn't mean he wanted to turn me into a robotic zombie with a perma-smile and no will of my own."

A shrewd brow rose. "You don't think he'd have tried?"

"No." But after a quick search of her feelings, she shrugged. "Maybe. To some degree. He's a little old-fashioned."

"He's the apple that fell from the tree, Sadie. You've met his parents, right?"

"Not since I've been back. His father's asthmatic. They moved to Santa Fe a year after Ty graduated from college."

"Daddy's choice, not Mommy's."

"Asthma is a medical condition, Lieutenant, not a choice. Where are you going with this, anyway, because you and I both know Ty's not stupid enough to believe he could have run roughshod over me, no matter how close the apple fell or where the parental tree currently lives?"

"You said it yourself, he still loves you."

"I also said he's not in love with me."

"It's a small step from one to the other."

"It's a huge step from love to obsession, which I realize now is what you've been hinting at since this conversation began. Ty's a straight guy. He doesn't drink, he doesn't obsess and he would never threaten someone he cared about."

Eli sent her a fathomless look. "Anyone can have a monster lurking inside, sweetheart. I was part of a team that brought down a serial killer three years ago. The killer ran a family supermarket in Yonkers. He did the baking himself every morning. He had a wife and three kids, and he came to Manhattan four times a year for conventions and ball games. Every time he left, there'd be at least two less women alive and working the streets."

She sighed. "Look, I can understand, even appreciate your mistrust. I just can't believe I'd have missed seeing it if Ty had a side to him as evil as the spirit that possessed your ancestor. How old was Ty when Laura died? Sixteen, right?"

"Just."

"But you were fourteen. Funny, when I was young, I thought you and Ty and Brady were the same age."

"Nope. I squeaked through grade school at the usual pace. Ty and Brady had a hate-hate relationship with a couple of our teachers and took a bit longer."

Amusement stirred. "Would one of those teachers be Mr. Hart?"

"Heard about him, huh?"

"Heard about and met." She widened meaningful eyes. "Your Mr. Hart is Orley's father."

ELI HAD TO look twice to be sure she was serious. "Orley's father? How the hell did I miss that?"

"Raccoon on the road," Sadie warned. "Eyes forward, Lieutenant, and I'll give you the easy answer. All girl babies born to Bellam females are given the Bellam surname. It's tradition. My dad's is a Winter, Molly's is a Prewitt and Orley's is a Hart. Orley claims he was nicer at home than at work, but my family's situation being what it was, we didn't interact a lot. Plus, I was ten years younger than her. Your situation being what *it* was, however, I'm surprised you were never forced to endure weekend dinners. Maybe your dad and hers didn't get along. Does your father hunt?"

"No."

"There you go, then."

Elbow propped, Eli ran a finger under his bottom lip. "I'm trying really hard here to picture no-Hart with a kid. Does he still live in the area?"

"Nope. North Dakota. Could be that's why Ty and Brady felt it was safe to take jobs here."

Eli geared down when the moon slipped behind a cloud and the wind booted up to kick the side of his truck. "Is it ever not blustery in this hollow?"

"Weather's a crapshoot once summer's done." She regarded the endless stretch of darkness ahead. "Molly's in love with Ty."

He allowed himself a brief smile. "Yeah, got that one from Orley. Six-inch heels. Ink spill on the sidewalk."

"Molly uses red ink and a raven's quill to do the place cards for her séances. She thinks it's more authentic."

"It's bizarre."

"Molly's a deep person, Eli, unlike—look out!"

He spied the glint of metal as she did and swung the truck into a wide arc. Not in time to avoid the obstruction, he realized instantly. The entire vehicle shuddered, then began to lurch. He glimpsed a five-foot boulder and heard a screech as the back end scraped across the rock face and sent them stuttering toward the edge of the ravine.

He didn't think, just grabbed Sadie's hand and helped her climb over the stick shift. "With me."

They jumped together from the still-rolling truck. Eli made sure she landed on top of him, then lost his grip and half slid, half tumbled over mud and weeds and slime. He flew through an air pocket and finally came to rest in a patch of cattails.

Between the wind in the trees and the thrum of blood in his ears, he needed a moment to get his mind and body back in sync. He took half of that moment and rolled onto his stomach. "Sadie?"

"Are we dead?"

Her voice came from the right. Working himself to his knees, Eli fought to steady his thoughts. Through the hair that dripped in his eyes, he caught a movement. When he pushed upright, however, the entire mud hole tilted. "Where are you?"

"I never want to do that again." The movement he'd noted became a squelch of wet weeds. "I can hear you, Eli, but all I see is mud and black."

On his feet now—not quite sure how he pulled it off with his muscles reduced to rubber—he made his way over to her, then lowered himself to a crouch and inspected her face. "Anything broken?"

"Other than my skull and tailbone, no. Or—I might have twisted my knee." She used both hands to swipe the hair from her eyes. "What in living hell did we hit back there?"

He glanced up. "It looked like a spike strip. Blew all four tires simultaneously."

"Spikes. In the middle of the road. Why?"

"Someone wanted to impede us, I imagine."

"Impede or impale. I thought…" She halted, swiveled her head. "Damn. Damn! We're in the bog, aren't we? Those spikes were only a few feet past the place where the pine tree came down. This is where we found Laura's body!"

Wrapping the fingers of one hand around the back of her neck, Eli stared into her eyes. "You're not going to get hysterical on me, are you?"

"Not sure. Maybe."

"Better if it could wait until we're out of here."

Little shivers ran through her, but she held his gaze in the faint wash of moonlight. "Where's your truck?"

"Probably ass up in the bog."

"Okay, well, you had to figure. At least we know the way out on foot. Or we did twenty years ago."

"Let's hope nothing's changed." He scoped the shadows that appeared to be multiplying around them. "Fog's rolling in."

"That's not possible." She plucked leaves from her hair. "There can't be fog when there's…" Pausing, she raised her eyes. "Where did the wind go?"

"Good question. Can you stand?"

"Stand, no problem. Walk, we'll see. Eli, wait." She tapped a fingernail lightly to his wrist. "We're being watched."

"Felt it. But watched isn't the problem."

"Of course not. That would be too simple." She was bending to examine her knee when a lethal-looking shaft whizzed over her head. "Uh…"

"Stay down, Sadie." Placing himself in front of her, Eli reached for his gun. "That was a crossbow arrow."

"Someone's using a crossbow at night?"

"Yeah." Eli held his gun barrel up. "Looks like the monster wants to hunt."

Chapter Thirteen

Every shadow became a monster to Sadie. Fighting through her fear, she sketched a quick mental map of Raven's Bog. Trouble was, with the exception of her recurring nightmares, she hadn't ventured deep into these woods since she was seven. And back then, no one had been shooting arrows at her with frightening skill and accuracy.

Eli pulled her to the ground several times as they ran. With good reason, she realized, as arrows began to embed themselves chest high in the tree trunks.

"Avoid the direct moonlight," he said from behind. "And don't trip."

A hiss formed. Of all the things he could have said, that was the least helpful. How could she not trip on a path bulging with roots from a bunch of gnarly old trees that reminded her of the faceless mob from her nightmare?

"Stop." Catching her shoulders, Eli halted her so abruptly her feet almost shot out from under her. "Behind the stump."

Sadie landed on her sore knee but didn't cry out. Instead, she strained to separate shadow from substance behind them.

Ground fog slunk through the rocks, slithered out of crevices and crawled up over the marsh vines. A few leaves rustled in the high branches, but otherwise the woods had gone silent. Unless she counted the drumbeat that was her heart, hammering against her ribs. Because that sound could drown out a rock band.

"Give me something," Eli invited their pursuer. "Put one damn foot wrong."

The moon disappeared behind thin fingers of cloud. Far in the distance, a frog croaked. Then another. And a third.

"Any chance you could shut them up?" Eli asked her.

"Is it possible they're communicating because the danger's gone?"

"Only in cartoons, Sadie. Someone who lays down a spike strip and follows up with a crossbow isn't likely to go away. Did you see anything before the first arrow flew past?"

She shook her head, and would have preferred not to think beyond that, except... "Military troops use crossbows to detonate land mines, right? Eli, Ty was in the military."

"Means nothing. Brady and I were competitive marksmen in high school archery."

"And many of the local residents are hunters, or come from hunting backgrounds."

Eli made a slow visual circle. "Don't discount the spike strip that landed us here, either."

"Who'd own...? Ah, Cal Kilgore."

"Man forges metal products." He nodded through the trees. "There. Someone moved. Looks like he's keeping his distance and circling."

Sadie's throat muscles tightened. "In that case, shouldn't we be leaving?"

"Ten seconds."

She tried not to grind her teeth. "If we head west, there's a cave that climbs up to the road. My great-grandfather took me through it when I was six."

"Knee okay to stand?"

"As I will, so mote it be." She worked up a humorless smile. "Means I'll take pain over death."

It also meant staying low and not disturbing the ground cover.

With only the occasional moonbeam to guide them, Sadie would have missed the cave if she hadn't spotted the haunted tree. The old oak was massive and had probably died before she'd been born. Yet it continued to stand, a home for ravens and, many believed, Hezekiah in his transformed state.

Like a wizard casting his spells, two large branches stretched upward, leaving the smaller limbs at the top to spread and curl like claws. There was even a black oval where a face might have been.

They had to backtrack twenty yards to locate the overgrown cave entrance.

"I'd sacrifice a year's pay for a flashlight," Sadie whispered once they'd wedged themselves inside. "Even a jarful of fireflies would help."

"In that case, you'll be pleased to hear I smoked until last summer."

"You have a lighter?"

"Yeah. Not sure how much juice it has left, though. Feel around the ground for a dry branch, the thinner the better."

"Lovely," she said, but took a bolstering breath, shoved up her sleeves and explored the ground with him.

"I should have grabbed an arrow," she muttered. "Except they're made of metal, not wood, aren't they? Taking us right back to Cal."

"He's reclimbing the list."

"Wouldn't he also be signing his name?"

"Some criminals think the most likely suspect becomes the least likely suspect in the eyes of the police," Eli said.

"Why?"

"No idea. Most likely's most likely. Investigators don't play games."

"Good to know. But staying in the criminal mind-set, who's the least likely suspect? Other than Rooney, who doesn't count because—well, duh."

"I thought you'd figure Ty for least likely."

"And I figured Ty was a given from your perspective.... Oh, wait. I found something."

She handed him a two-foot-long twig. "Six of one," she murmured. "Either we stumble along in the dark and risk breaking a leg, or we risk having whoever's after us see the flame."

Thankfully, no arrows flew out of the dark, and Sadie prayed all the crunching footsteps she heard belonged to them. Then she turned a corner, walked into a spiderweb and spent the next minute trying to keep the scream that leaped into her throat from escaping.

It frustrated her that she also had to battle a strong urge to grab Eli's gun and start firing into the shadows behind them.

"Don't think so hard, Sadie," Eli advised. "You'll only mess up your mind more than it already is. You need to focus on putting one foot in front of the other until we're out of here."

She trudged another fifty yards up the sloping ground before deciding to hell with it and declaring over her shoulder, "I want to have sex with you, Eli."

Snagging the belt of her trench coat, he drew her to a halt and lowered his mouth to her ear. "Say that again, sweetheart, this time without the underlying threat of you turning me into a lizard if my answer isn't to your liking."

Pushing the burning twig he held to one side, she turned to face his glittering eyes. "I want to have sex with you, Eli,

when we're out of this cave, out of the hollow and somewhere, anywhere, warm and safe and dry." Even knowing
her timing was way off, she pressed her hips to the front of
his jeans. "I don't want to die, but even more than that, I
don't want to die and never know what it would have been
like to make love with you."

She saw the glitter deepen. "I'd want to make love to
you even with the threat of life as a lizard hanging over
my head." His gaze dropped to her mouth, then rose. "No
matter what my form, though, Sadie, I won't let anyone
hurt you." Capturing her chin, he grazed her lips with his
and added a soft "Especially not me."

"KISSING ME, THEN GOING all enigmatic cop isn't going to
get you out of explaining what you meant." Sadie ducked
under a rough protrusion and immediately had her face
slapped by an embedded weed. "You'll also never convince
me that you're a threat to my life, so—oh, good, there's
the opening—if you're not into sex, just say so and we'll
leave it at that."

"Find a foothold" was all he said, and gave her a boost
from behind. "When you reach the exit, move aside and
let me go first."

He had the gun, he was the cop—it made sense. But
Sadie was irked enough to say nothing while he pushed
through the underbrush and took a long look around.

"We're about a mile south of the bog," he revealed when
he returned. "Maybe a hundred yards from the road."

Using an elastic band from the pocket of her trench, she
secured her hair. "That would put us midway between the
Cove and the Hollow. Do we flip a coin?"

"Anyone we want to talk to should be down at Two
Toes Joe's Bar."

"The Cove it is. Eli." She caught his arm. "Once we're

on the road, we're exposed. The wind blew most of the clouds away, and the fog's not thick enough to obscure the moon."

"Which is why you'll be carrying my backup and trying to reach Ty on your cell phone."

She took the gun and pulled her iPhone from her pocket. A rueful smile appeared when the screen lit up. "Second duh of the night. We could have used this as a light source in the cave."

"Fire worked well enough. If we'd killed your battery, there'd have been no way for us to call for help later."

"You didn't think of it, either, huh?"

He sent her a distant grin. "Other things on my mind, sweetheart."

It felt as if the night wanted to close in around them. Sadie slammed a firm lid on the more insidious aspects of her dream. No point making everything worse. If anything could be worse.

"Tell me what you're thinking," she said as they approached the narrow strip of road. "I can hear your mind clicking, but I can't read it."

"Oh, I imagine you could if you tried."

"You kissed me to shut me up."

"Skip ahead, Sadie."

"Any of those dozen or so arrows we avoided in the bog could have hit you as easily as me. More easily, in fact, because you were shielding me."

"Which I'll do every time, so lose the accusing tone and stay on track."

She tapped the phone screen with her thumb, glanced behind them. "Obsessed person transforms into monster. Monster's pissed at me for—what? Not understanding his message?"

"Go with that."

"He's also pissed at you for coming to the Hollow and getting in his way. So he's decided to eliminate both of us for his—host?"

"Good a description as any."

"Once we're gone, the monster retreats, the host mourns and soon enough, life resumes its normal rhythm." She ran the idea a few times. "Going back to Laura, and assuming Cal's not the killer, that could explain why he's not dead. He and Laura broke up. He ceased to be a problem. The monster set his sights on Laura alone. Am I babbling?"

"A little. It's better than freaking."

Following his lead, she glanced into the darkness behind them. "Why do we keep looking over our shoulders?"

"Someone's back there."

Her fingers tightened on her phone. "I was really hoping that was my imagination."

"Keep calling, Sadie."

"I can walk, talk and check an i-screen at the same time. It's a dead zone until we begin the descent into the—whoa—Cove!" With no forewarning, she found herself airborne as Eli tackled her into a ditch. "What now?" she demanded, climbing off him.

"Gleam of metal. Keep quiet."

She obliged and listened. And, dammit, heard footsteps. Stealthy footsteps, squishing on the shoulder.

"How far back does this ditch run?" Eli asked.

"Maybe fifty yards. Wait." She gripped his wrist. "He's stopped."

"Noticed." Pivoting, he took hold of her arms. "I need you to stay right here."

"While you walk into an arrow? Because you know that's what he wants…." She trailed off, raised her head. "I hear a car. No, a truck. It's coming from the Cove."

To her relief—and, she suspected, Eli's annoyance—the

engine grew louder. When the fog lamps came into view, he hoisted himself from the ditch and flagged the driver down with his badge.

The man who stopped was a farmer named Ray. Their weapons didn't faze him, but one look at her, covered in mud and sludge, with leaves and bark clinging to her hair, had his thick eyebrows winging up and laughter gurgling in his throat. Until she gave him the short version of their story. Then he reached behind him for a rifle.

"You and me could take a walk," he said around her to Eli.

"Do you have a night-vision scope?"

"Three of 'em." He scratched his throat. "Sorry to say, they're at home."

"Would it matter if they weren't?" Sadie turned to Eli. "The guy was behind us. He'll know we got a ride. He also knows the area, because I didn't hear him behind us in the cave. Every witchy sense I possess tells me that he and his crossbow have vanished into the night. We can drive slowly, keep an eye open for anything suspicious, but you know it's done for now. We're safe, and he's gone. We should be grateful for small—well, okay, big—favors."

Eli scanned the road. "Big and small are relative terms, Sadie. Small picture, we're safe for the moment. Big one, the killer's still out there. And we have no idea who he is or where he'll surface again. The only thing we can be sure of is that his homicidal alter ego won't stop until it does what it came out of hibernation to do."

HE WOKE UP facedown on the bathroom floor, with the shower running and the spray gone icy. Every part of his body ached, but his head most of all. Crawling to the tub, he prayed the cold water would shock some clarity into his brain.

Even with the haze dispersing, he couldn't remember the night. He knew he'd opened a can of beans for dinner, thought he'd eaten most of them, plus coffee and a few stale cookies. But that's where it ended. His mind went blank after the first bite of gingersnap.

Okay, back up. He'd been tired. He'd drifted off. Then what? What grim horror had unfolded while he slept?

His palms felt damp. The skin on his neck prickled. It wasn't morning yet, not quite. First light was coming, but slowly, like the panic that was starting to pitch and roll inside him.

"What did I do?" he whispered to the walls. "What did we do?"

The bathroom held no answers, so he shut off the water and grabbed a towel when he left.

There was no sign of blood. Maybe it wasn't too terrible. Swallowing the grit in his throat, he moistened his lips. He should contact Sadie. Yes, he needed to stay calm and ascertain her status.

Ascertain her status? Whose thought was that? And why couldn't he remember?

Feeling like a man after a weekend drunk, he walked with his face buried in the towel. When he walked into a table, he lowered his hands and forced his bleary eyes to travel from point to point in the room. Chair to window. Window to floor. Floor to door.

When they stopped, so did his heart, for several long seconds. Then it started to gallop.

He stared, sweat dribbling, at the entryway, at the shoes he wore for special occasions. And the layers of green-brown mud that coated them.

Chapter Fourteen

"Word has it the fights at Joe's bar got out of hand last night." Molly picked up and shook the bottle of Tylenol on Sadie's kitchen counter. "When all was said and done—long after midnight, I'm told—Rooney called Ty, who never showed, and reamed him out. Ty called Brady, also a no-show, and on down a twisty, turny path, until sometime around 2:00 a.m., our great-grandfather called me from the north woods. Among other things, he wants you to listen to your landline and cell phone messages more often. Same memo to Eli.… Er, where was I?"

"You lost me after 'the fights at Joe's bar got out of hand.'" At the table, Sadie raised her forehead from her arms. Molly had invaded her kitchen at 6:00 a.m., on her one and only day off after a night of pure hell that had not resulted in her and Eli having hot sex or even a reasonable facsimile thereof. "Why are you telling me this?"

"Because Rooney's upset that you weren't there wearing your journalist's hat. Your only saving grace is that he's miffed at several of us for doing other life things when he believes we should have been drinking Joe's gross beer and throwing up in the bathroom between bouts. Do you want coffee?'

Sadie propped her chin in her palms. "Do ravens have feathers? My guess is Joe's was packed to the rafters, and everyone in attendance snapped a dozen or more photos with his or her phone. My assistant—" she emphasized the word "—will have plenty to choose from when she opens her morning emails."

"I noticed you didn't get home until close to midnight." Molly measured out the ground beans. "Would that be Eli's doing?"

How much should she reveal? Sadie wondered. "Eli and I had an incident on the Hollow Road. By the time we got to the Cove, we were wet and muddy and not very happy. We spent close to an hour trying to locate Ty, only to be told he was still in Raven's Hollow. So, back we went. At a snail's pace, though, because Eli wanted to see if he could locate his truck."

Molly stopped her measuring spoon halfway to the machine. "Eli lost his truck?"

"Long story. Short answer? Yes. With it went my camera bag and all the pictures I'd taken of Ben Leamer's corn maze—which I flatly refuse to walk through again after discovering a wolf spider the size of Solomon on my coat sleeve yesterday afternoon."

"I have shots of the maze," Molly told her. "Lots of them. In a way, you could say I helped design it."

Sadie slid her eyes sideways and up. "Say what?"

"More accurately, I helped Brady, who helped Ben design it." She returned to her task. "Think, Sadie. Brady's a vet. He takes care of Ben Leamer's livestock and pets. He spends a lot of time at the farm. Ben asked for help, Brady made suggestions and when we—Brady and I— drove into Bangor together for medical supplies, I did a little tweaking for him." Her mouth tipped up into a rare smile. "I remember Orley smoldering over that trip, because it left her alone at the clinic. According to her, hell broke loose that afternoon, and being a complete putz at channeling her emotions, she blamed me for taking Brady away. Put another X in the 'I hate Molly' column. Did Eli find his truck?"

"What? No. It's in the bog somewhere, though, has to be."

She glanced up to find Molly gaping at her. "Why is Eli's truck in the bog?"

"Have you ever heard of a spike strip?"

"No."

"Picture spikes on a chain meeting tires on a road. Going back to Ben's maze for a minute—who designed the layout of the paths?"

"I imagine Ben did. Ty warned him to keep things on the low side of terrifying, but I think Ben added a few more figures after he—Ty—did his walk-through."

"Ty did a walk-through?"

"You sound like a broken record, Sadie."

"I know. Why didn't Ben tell me any of this?"

Molly's eyebrows came together. "Because it wasn't important?"

"Right." Sadie regarded the hissing coffeemaker. "Right. It wasn't—isn't." Was it? "I need to wake up more." And sift and sort and process. She opted to change the subject. "Do you need help with the séance?"

"Not on the inside. You know what they say about too many cooks. But you should probably know Ty will be there. Ty—Eli." She made a spacing motion with her hands. "I'll seat them far apart. I was going to invite Cal Kilgore, too, but I don't know how to reach him, do you?"

"Not without dodging bullets." Sadie grinned. "Rooney might know."

"Why would Rooney know how to contact a metal maker from the north woods?"

"Because being so tied up with his maze, one or two

of Ben Leamer's other ventures have been shunted to the back burner lately."

"Are you being cryptic on purpose?"

"At six in the morning, absolutely not. Talk to Rooney." Pushing away from the table, Sadie headed for the now-spitting machine. "Why do you want Cal at the séance, Molly?" It struck her as she reached for the pot. "Oh, damn. Tell me you're not going to do what I suddenly have a horrible feeling you're going to do."

Her cousin linked and twisted her fingers. "I have to do it, don't I? I saw the writing on your entry wall. I also heard you and Eli talking. I know what you're thinking. What's happening to you is a lot like what happened to Laura." She worked up a smile. "Think of it this way. We're making a phone call. A very long distance phone call."

It only took from predawn until noon to get his truck out of the hellhole that was Raven's Bog. Cursing and snarling by turns, Eli inspected the scraped and dented body. But when he saw the shredded tires, it hit him what he could have lost if even one small part of last night's horror show had gone down differently.

"I have to say, this is much worse than the tree." Brady circled while Eli crouched to inspect the rear axle. "Is Ty looking into what happened, or are you taking it on yourself?"

"What, you think he'll stay out of it if I ask nicely?"

"I think I don't want to wind up in the middle of things."

"In that case—" Ty slid down the gentlest portion of the embankment "—you should consider removing yourself right now. Arrows, Eli? Someone shot arrows at Sadie last night?"

Eli regarded him from the ground. "That was act two, Ty. The first was even more fun."

"Right, the spike line." He made a show of searching the ground. "Funny, I don't see one lying around anywhere, but your tires are screwed, I'll give you that."

Shaking his head in mild amusement, Brady leaned on the banged-up box. "Don't mind me. I'll just stand here and try to figure out what I'm going to tell Rooney when he blasts me again for not showing up at the fights last night."

In spite of everything, Eli could still chuckle. "Consider yourself lucky. I got my encore blast before I was fully awake."

Ty's eyes shot hot spikes. "And just where were you, cousin, when this encore blasting occurred?"

"Where you probably think," Eli returned. "Or close to it."

"What the hell does that mean?"

"Oh, come on, Ty," Brady called out. "You're not dense. He was at Bellam Manor, but not in Sadie's bed. At least not when he talked to Rooney."

Eli wiped his hands on an old rag. "You're enjoying this, aren't you?"

Brady shrugged. "Fair's fair. I had to euthanize a sixteen-year-old Lab late yesterday afternoon. I need some enjoyment. Having said that, I'll do what I can to make Brick's tow truck work for me. Just remember, hauling's not my strong suit."

Ty's scowl became a sneer. "Couldn't get either one of the Majerki brothers to help you, huh?"

Eli tossed the rag. "Is that the burning question, or would you rather have the details on my night at Bellam Manor?"

Ty's neck went red. "I don't see a tail and long ears, so neither of the resident witches turned you into a donkey. Sadie'd say anything else was between you and her. Speaking of, is she someplace safe?"

"She's at the manor with Molly."

"Who's not exactly a ninja. Do you ever think of any-one but yourself?"

"About as much as you do. It's covered," he said before his cousin could protest further. "She's safe."

"Guess I'll have to take that on faith."

"Guess you will."

Ty showed his teeth. "Where's the spike chain?"

"Long gone, unless whoever planted it is a complete fool. Not very likely."

"Sloppy's been known to happen in cases like this."

"Yeah? How many cases like this have you known?"

His cousin moved a shoulder. "I poked into Laura's death some after I came to the office."

"And?"

Ty's grin fell just short of feral. "If I told you that, you'd have nothing to challenge your slick investigative skills, would you?"

"Sounds like he turned up a big fat zero to me." Brady used the heavy lift chain to get Eli's vehicle airborne. "Is a spike line what it sounds like?"

"Pretty much." Eli's stomach clenched when the hoist bobbled and almost dropped his truck back into the bog. "Know anybody who has one?"

"No, but Ben Leamer's got a long, spiky, rake-like thing out at his farm."

Ty snorted. "Why would old Ben want to wreck Eli's truck?"

"Just answering the question." Brady disengaged the safety chain. "Ben's whatever-it-is is the only object I can think of that's got the potential for a wicked bite."

"Unless you count Rooney's signature tea." Eli hopped onto the flatbed. "Let's get this done, okay?"

Leaving Brady to secure the front of the vehicle, he

worked on the back while Ty strode around and did his best to be a complete ass.

Would he be an ass if their situations were reversed? Eli wondered. And he had to admit that, yeah, he might.

"Is this Sadie's?" Fighting the door open, his cousin reached for a mud-encrusted black leather bag. "Unless I'm wrong and it's yours, I hope there was nothing important inside." He unzipped it to rummage through the contents. "Camera, lenses, iPad, shorthand notes—all dry and un-broken." His smile could have cut glass. "Lucky her." He kicked the dented door as closed as it would go. "Not so lucky you. Go long, Lieutenant."

Eli nabbed the bag halfway to the slimy water. "Nice of you to zip it back up."

"Nice isn't what I'm feeling at the moment. In fact, what I'm feeling is in the mood to participate in one of those bor-derline legal fights Rooney is forever arranging behind my back. Problem is, we're nowhere near Two Toes Joe's bar."

Eli glanced into the camera bag. "Mud works for me." He rezipped as he spoke and only looked down again when the teeth snagged. The corner of a folded paper stuck out, but it wasn't until he drew the pull tab back and spied the red lettering that his blood ran cold.

Ty's voice faded to an irritating buzz. Freeing the caught corner, Eli removed a sheet of paper that ran a full two feet in length. The words slashed across it were like acid in his system.

While the man's away
The monster can play.

"WHY DOES THIS monster hate me so much? Or at all? Be-cause it can't control the side of itself that's got a weird obsession with me?" Sadie dipped under a low branch in the woods near Bellam Manor. "We need to find haw-thorn leaves."

"Let me know when we do." Eli held the branch up. "Jealousy's not uncommon with a split personality, Sadie. One side often wants what the other side has."

"Yes, but that's not the case here, is it? The nonmonster doesn't actually have. He only wants."

"And the monster doesn't want the nonmonster to get. Simple solution? Eliminate the prize."

Sadie studied Molly's wish list for the séance. Bendable willow branches, wild lavender, fennel, thyme and rose-mary from the old garden. "The writing didn't change, Eli. The paper was long and folded, like the one Laura found in her gym bag, but the writing in my message was con-sistent. Creepy, but consistent. Theory?"

"Cal's trying to throw us off track."

Stepping into an overgrown herb garden outside the original Bellam graveyard, she snipped some thyme, sniffed the leaves and dropped them into a paper bag. "Then why did Cal tell us he was ambidextrous? He didn't have to. Obviously, the police missed that fact during their investigation into Laura's death."

"Obviously, the police were out of their depth and re-ceived very little peripheral help when it came to Laura's case."

She tilted her head. "Hate to point this out, Lieutenant, but you're not receiving any peripheral help, either. Or looking to bring any in as far as I can tell."

The gleam in his eyes made her breath hitch in a ridic-ulously exciting way.

"One click of a computer key, and I have a wealth of information at my fingertips. The trick is to sort through the clutter until you hit pay dirt. The coroner's report on

Laura's homicide said she was struck from behind by a left-handed person."

"Meaning she felt comfortable enough to turn her back on the killer?"

"Or she was forced to turn it. Left-handed's the gold, Sadie."

"Yes, I got that." She sighed. "And now you're going to ask me how many of the men I've interacted with between the Hollow and the Cove are left-handed. My answer is, not Ty."

"Not Brady, either."

She laughed. "Well, hell, Eli, I can hardly read what Brady writes with his right hand." She paused midsnip. "Wait a second. Rewind. You think Brady could have a monster living inside him?"

"Brady, Two Toes Joe, Brick from the tow yard, his brother, one of Ty's deputies."

She cut a sprig of lavender, but instead of bagging it, she stood, twirled the stem in her fingers and strolled slowly toward him. "That's quite the voice you have there, Lieutenant Blume. Of experience, I mean." Touching her tongue to her upper lip, she dropped her gaze for a meaningful second. "It's very—sexy."

His eyes caught and held hers. "You had to know my last relationship didn't work out well on either side."

She hooked a finger in his waistband. "Gathered that."

"I almost hurt someone I cared about."

And tugged. "Almost being the operative word."

"I'm not going to do the same thing to you."

"I'm not going to let you do the same thing to me—whatever it is or was." Reaching for his oh-so-tempting mouth, she asked, "Any more pointless objections?"

"Yeah, but to hell with them," he muttered, and pulled

her so hard against him that she could feel every muscle in his body, from sleek biceps to tantalizing arousal.

It felt good, she thought, as pleasure hummed through her veins, not to be balanced on the high wire of her nerves. If only for a few minutes, she wanted to let the heat build and the fever, which was a wicked blend of need and desire, take hold.

The second Eli's mouth captured hers, his tongue plunged inside to feast.

He tasted like the night, like darkness and danger. The restless hunger that had been part of him for as long as Sadie could remember flowed out of him and into her. It made her blood pump and her skin tingle.

She breathed in, then blissfully out. This was how she'd felt when they'd danced that first night in Boston. In that single heady moment she'd known with absolute certainty she wouldn't be marrying Ty.

Cupping her face in his hands, Eli deepened the kiss, then ran his fingers lightly over her shoulders and arms until they found her breasts. She moaned, and the moan became a low purr as his thumbs grazed the nipples under her T-shirt and bra. His lips moved from her mouth to her jaw and along the column of her throat.

"Gonna melt in a minute," she warned, but didn't know if she spoke the words or merely thought them.

"Already have," he murmured against her neck.

Letting her head bow back, Sadie savored the sensations sweeping through her. Desire mixed with the heat that spiraled upward from her belly. Breathless, she took a moment to revel in the kind of liquid need she'd never expected to feel. Wasn't entirely sure she'd wanted to feel.

She dug her fingers into his upper arms, felt lean muscle and hard bone and knew, *knew* she should push herself away. Should never have started this in the first place, because…

When he took her mouth again, the thought simply turned to dust and scattered.

He awakened every one of her sleeping senses. Wanting him even closer, she slid her hands upward, until her fingers were impossibly tangled in his hair. Rough bark scraped her back, and the first drops of rain hit her cheeks. She could feel him hard and pulsing against her. All she had to do was jump up, wrap her legs around his hips and let gravity and hunger take them down into the remains of the flower bed. The setting was perfect, and the thunder that rumbled over the hollow merely layered anticipation over desire.

She spied it before she sank all the way into him. A misty shadow that wasn't a shadow but a solid figure. Like the zealots from her nightmare, it wore a black cloak and held something in its hand.

Dragging her mouth free, Sadie managed a breathless "Gun!"

Eli reacted so swiftly she barely noticed the move. Shoving her to the ground, he pulled his Police Special and spun into a kneeling crouch.

The figure's first bullet struck the tree behind them. The second—no idea. The third blew one of the herb bags apart.

Crawling to him, Sadie felt for Eli's backup and tugged it free. There was a fence, a crooked line of pickets between him and the now-secreted shooter. Not much of a shield in her opinion.

Flat on the ground, her breath held to the point of discomfort, she squeezed the trigger. The gun kicked pain up to her elbows, but she continued to squeeze off shots.

She might have heard some thrashing at that point, and

maybe she glimpsed receding black, but if she was honest, the whole thing had become a jumble of sight and sound. So she continued to pump out shots until she heard nothing but empty clicks.

Before the last echo died, Eli was up and gone. Sadie dropped her face onto her extended arms and breathed. She heard the double tone from her phone but ignored it until her senses rebooted. When they did, she raised her head and scoured the nearby woods.

There was nothing. No sound, no movement, no clue as to where Eli had gone.

"Just once," she muttered in frustration, "I'd like an easy answer."

She was debating her limited options when her phone beeped again. Preoccupied, she dug it from her jacket pocket.

More raindrops plopped onto her head, and the thunder that shook the flower bed and grave markers was creeping closer. High in the trees, ravens cawed. One of them swooped in for a landing on a tippy picket.

"Give me all the evil looks you want, pal." She went to her message app. "After what I've gone through lately, I'm immune."

The bird cawed noisily, but Sadie didn't hear it, or anything. The text message that appeared on the screen stopped her breath and sent a shaft of pure terror into her heart.

I WASN'T SHOOTING AT YOU!

Chapter Fifteen

"People don't vanish," Ty maintained an hour later. "Outsmart other people, yes, but even on Bellam land, they can't twitch up a broomstick and fly off into the ether."

"I was thinking more along the lines of jumping into a rabbit hole. Or a cave, like the one Sadie and I used to climb out of the bog." Eli flicked through files in his cousin's private office. "Don't you have any maps that predate the nineteen fifties?"

"The *Chronicle* might." Sadie glanced up from her iPhone. "There are a lot of boxes in the basement. I can look tomorrow. We really should be leaving for the manor soon, if we want…" Pausing, she peered around Ty's arm at the veterinary clinic across the street. "Orley's pulling in," she told them. "Back in a sec."

"Bad mood happening here, Sadie." A scowling Orley climbed from her car. "Brady and I just chased down a deer with an arrow in its hind leg. We had to use a tranquilizer dart on it. The tranq worked, but naturally the deer toppled into a pile of dung and had to be worked on where it lay."

"Is it all right?"

"It will be. Gorgeous animal. A buck."

"In that case, and given that you like animals a thousand times better than humans, how could saving a deer put you in a bad mood?"

Orley bared her teeth. "I'm wearing my Gucci suede boots. I swear, if I find out who launched that arrow, I'm going to shoot him in the leg and leave him to bleed in the woods." Her grimace morphed into a weary expulsion of breath when a truck creaked to a halt behind her. "Dr. Dolittle in the flesh."

Climbing from his truck, Brady shouldered his medical bag and picked up a crossbow arrow.

"I hate hunters," Orley muttered. "My dad hunts, so opposite sides of the fence there, but at least he knows you can't kill an animal by aiming for the ass end. Any poacher worth his salt should know that, too."

"You can't be sure it was a poacher, Orley." Brady followed Sadie's narrowed stare to the arrow. "What? I'm not the nitwit who pulled the trigger."

"Sorry, knee-jerk. Where was the deer?"

Orley picked at one of her ruined boots. "In the hollow."

"Near Raven's Bog?"

"Within spitting distance. Why?"

"Can't write an article without all the facts."

Brady arched a surprised brow. "An arrow in the haunch of a deer's newsworthy?"

"It is today." She wiggled her fingers. "Can I see the arrow?"

"You must be having one very slow news day." But Brady relinquished the metal shaft. "And here they come—the never-gonna-be Bobbsey Twins."

Sadie heard Ty's snort of disgust at the same time Eli's arm dropped across her shoulders.

"Might want to keep that arrow away from your ex, sweetheart," he murmured, "or it could wind up in an innocent back."

Ty sneered. "Now, why would I want to impale the town vet? Hand it, Sadie."

At a small nod from Eli, she complied.

"Ah, right, got it." Brady's face cleared. "You think this is one of the arrows that was shot at you and Eli on Sunday night. Instead of hitting its intended target, it hit a deer."

"Always possible," Eli agreed.

"I want to talk to Cal." Ty twirled the arrow. "Are you sure you didn't get a disclaimer after the attack in the bog, Sadie?"

Still out of sorts, Orley raised her gaze from her ruined boots. "Since when do would-be murderers put out disclaimers?"

Sadie shrugged. "Someone in a black cloak and hood put one out earlier today. He was shooting at Eli and me near the graveyard at Bellam Manor. Shooter rabbited. A few minutes later, I got a text. He said the bullets weren't meant for me."

Orley snorted. "Sounds like someone's head is seriously messed up. No offense, cous."

"None taken."

Brady ran a hand over his face. "What about the attack in the bog?"

Eli watched Ty play with the arrow. "I think whoever was behind that wanted both of us dead."

"You're not in the guy's head, though, are you?" Ty looked up with a level expression. "You're also not on your own turf, so maybe you're reading the whole thing wrong, or at least coming at it from the wrong direction. I know the Hollow and the Cove. I know how the people here think, and what they think and why."

"Ty, Eli grew up here, too... Uh, right." Palms out, Brady backed off. "You two hash it out. Triangles aren't my..."

"Eli, that's Cal in the truck at the corner!" Sadie grabbed the wrist still draped over her shoulder. "What's he doing here? No, wait, don't spook... Why do I even talk?" she wondered, as first Eli, then Ty, then Cal bolted. "It's like being in a *Rambo* movie. Séance starts at seven, Orley," she called back as she ran for her Land Rover.

Eli was already inside. "Forget it," he said, and started to slam the lock down.

But Sadie got the door open a split second faster and climbed in. "My vehicle, my decision. Go, or you'll be fighting Ty for road space."

He slanted her a dark look but didn't argue further. Couldn't because Ty fishtailed his cruiser around the corner and set off after Cal with a screech of tires and a series of short bursts on the siren.

Sadie gripped the dash with one hand and the side of Eli's seat with the other. "Any chance you two could work together on this?"

"Any way you know of to transmit that request to Ty?"

"He has a cell…."

"Any way that'll work?"

He had her there. She kept Cal's gray truck in sight. "If we assume he's heading back to the woods, you could take the Post Road and cut him off at the junction before the hollow. Then if Ty squeezes him from behind…" She made a dubious motion. "It could work."

But it didn't. Instead of cornering their quarry, Eli wound up in a near collision with Ty's cruiser, leaving Cal to bump through the junction and roar away on a rocky path few mountain goats would attempt.

Recognizing the expression on Eli's face, Sadie covered the gearshift with her hand. "Please don't. I can't afford a new vehicle, and I'm not insured for extreme off-road adventures. Cal knows these woods better than we do. Plus, we have his home address."

When the light in his eyes didn't diminish, she did the

only thing she could think of. She reached over the console, took his face in her hands and set her mouth on his.

Because she only meant to distract him, the sudden burst of heat surprised her. It also caused every thought in her head to wink out.

A dazzled "Wow" was the best she could manage when she eased herself away. "I didn't expect...hmm."

His lips curved. "Serious understatement. But as long as we're here."

He had her over the console and straddling him before her brain restarted.

The hunger bottled inside her shot need and adrenaline into her veins. Bunching his jacket, she let her eyes sparkle into his. "As first times go, this wouldn't be my setting of choice, but it's better than—oh, damn, Ty!"

The memory of the near collision had her whipping her head around. "He's—gone," she realized in relief. Then frowned. "Why is he gone?"

Eli rested his forehead against her hair. "He didn't go after Cal, if that's what you're thinking."

"Oh, I'm not up to thinking quite yet. My head's still buzzing, and I'm in kind of a nice place physically." She shimmied her butt on his lap. "However..."

Employing every scrap of self-restraint she possessed, Sadie climbed off and dropped back into her seat. "Bet he saw us."

"If he didn't, he should be declared legally blind." Moving carefully, Eli grinned. "Message received. No wild rides."

"Only where my Land Rover's concerned. Anything else is fair game." When her gaze drifted to the dash clock, her eyes widened. "Is that the time? We need to go. Molly sets a strict schedule."

"For a séance? Sorry, sweetheart, I have to say again, your cousin's very strange."

"Strange is the middle name of every Bellam and Blume descendant I know. Molly schedules bathroom breaks, Eli. She'll follow through whether we're there or not. And if the monster who wants me, you, or me and you dead shows up—very likely—the last thing I want to do is not be there and have him decide to vent his rage on people I care about."

Eli regarded the brooding sky. "Okay, we'll go through with it. But I want to check out Molly's apartment top to bottom before we start."

"It'll be Nola's apartment." Sadie flicked the ends of her hair. "In order to achieve the proper atmosphere, Molly does her summoning in what our family believes was Nola Bellam's inner sanctum."

"Great. Anything else I don't want to know?"

"You decide. At her last séance, two years ago, after Molly commanded the spirit in question to signal her presence by knocking three times, we heard three consecutive taps at the window."

"Signals can be rigged, Sadie."

"Not done yet. Nola's room is on the third floor of the manor. When we opened the shutters, we found a raven sitting on the sill."

"Which is unusual because?"

"He had a locket at his feet, which belonged to the dead woman. A locket no one had supposedly seen since before the spirit being summoned passed on."

"Uh-huh." Now his lips twitched. "Can I assume this locket belonged to your ancestor?"

"Ten points to you, Lieutenant."

"What was inside? A miniature painting of Hezekiah?"

Unable to resist, Sadie leaned over the console and used

her index finger to trace the line of his jaw. "Not quite. There were two locks of hair inside, one red, one black. And beneath them was a tiny piece of paper that read:

Whosoever shall open my locket

Will find no peace.

In this life or the next."

Eli curled his fingers around her neck. "Gotta be more to it than that. Who opened the locket?"

She touched her mouth to his in the lightest of kisses. "You already know the answer. I did."

SADIE DIDN'T BELIEVE in portents or omens, never had. However, a séance in her ancestral home in the throes of the chaos that was unfolding around her, had her wishing she'd taken that job at the *New York Times* after all.

She opted to wear traditional black—an ankle-skimming dress with a deep V, long pointy sleeves and just cling enough to bolster her slightly battered confidence.

She got a major boost when she opened the front door of the manor. Eli's eyes glinted dangerously even as Rooney hobbled in to wedge himself between them.

Beaming with delight, the old man wrapped his bony fingers around her upper arms. "Nola won't be putting in an appearance with one of her progeny looking as drop-dead beautiful as you do tonight, Sadie Bellam." He inhaled deeply. "Smell like a dream, too. Hope your cousin's got a standby spirit up her witchy sleeve."

"It wouldn't surprise me." She looked at Eli, then past him into the teaming rain before escorting Rooney slowly up the stairs to the third floor.

"No need to fuss," he assured her as she seated him. "You just make sure the tea's hot and the whiskey that makes it drinkable isn't of the soda pop variety. On the off

chance my heart stops from fright, I'll be needing something stronger than chamomile to jump-start it."

Sadie set a hip on the round table, crossed her arms
and regarded him with a semihumorous expression. "I
thought you were a firm believer in all the local lore, not
merely your own."

"Oh, I believe, young Sadie, but I also know shinola
when I see it. Molly's got the trappings down pat. Hanging plants, rocks and crystals scattered, participants seated
where she chooses, mood music for effect, candles for
light. It all looks, sounds and smells perfect, but is it real
or just a show for the tourists?" He tapped his nose. "One
way or another, with a hundred-plus years under my belt,
I'll sniff out the truth. Now, let's get down to basics." His
cane hit the floor between his knees. "Firstly, are you or
my great-grandson gonna tell your favorite centenarian
why I got a half-crazed phone call from Brick Majerki late
this afternoon? And secondly, does a man's heart actually
need to stop before he can get a mug of tea in this house?"

On cue, Orley slammed a tray holding four pots and several mugs onto the table, growled out a hello and marched
off.

"Green pot's yours," Sadie stage-whispered to Rooney.
"Hey, Jerk," she said to the man just entering the room.
"Rooney here was asking about your brother. Seeing as
Brick's so fearful of all things Bellam, I never expected
to see either of you at the manor."

The big man scratched his cheek. "Well, I'm not Brick,
now, am I, Sadie? The story of *Hansel and Gretel* sent little
bro under the bed for a week. Me, I only cared about sinking my teeth into a big chunk of that gingerbread house."

Sadie had known Jerk and Brick for two years. When
they weren't hauling or tearing apart dead vehicles, they
liked to tinker with old machines. They'd been tinkering

with the printing presses at the *Chronicle* since before her uncle retired.

Rooney winked at her. "Maybe Molly's crystal ball's on the fritz and she called Jerk here to fix it. Even she knows you'd never get the Brickman within a mile of this place on a night like this, not for all the whiskey in Ben Leamer's—"

"Corn," Sadie inserted smoothly. Her eyes found Eli in the doorway. "Not for all the corn in Ben Leamer's maze, Rooney. Is Molly's crystal ball on the fritz, Jerk?"

Brick's brother grinned. "Can't say as I know why she asked me to come."

"I didn't ask you to come," Molly said from behind him. "You asked me if there was an empty seat."

"And then you asked him to come," Sadie put in. "Which is why he's here, undoubtedly against his brother's wishes, but hey, you have to go your own way, right, Jerk?"

The big man poured himself and Rooney a mug of tea. "I've seen that gleam in your eyes before, Sadie. You wanna punch someone in the balls, Eli's made the rounds and he's heading this way right now."

Rooney clinked his mug to Jerk's. "If I were you, Sadie, I'd leave the ball punching to Ty. He looks hissy as a snake, don't you think?"

"Oh, this night's going to be so much fun," she predicted, then twirled in a half circle. "What about you, Lieutenant Blume? Are you up for a little fun?"

"Only if the word *fun* has suddenly become a synonym for debacle." He snagged a mouthful of Rooney's tea before propelling her into a corner crammed with dusty, sheet-covered furniture. "This gathering is a ticking time bomb. You should be as far away from it as possible."

She sent him a guileless look. "Your suggestion might have worked out better if you'd mentioned it earlier. That way, instead of being here, Jerk could be playing pool with Brick, who's completely freaked at the thought of his brother participating in a Bellam séance." She pushed a meaningful fist into his stomach. "How long has Jerk been guard-dogging me?"

Catching her balled fingers, Eli brought them to his lips. "Since you and Orley went into Ben Leamer's corn maze and you came out with the news that a monster had been added to the mix."

Part of her softened, couldn't help it. Another part resented his need-to-know attitude. "I thought we'd established that all murderers have monsters living inside them."

"They do, but I sense a growing separation of entities with this guy."

"We've established that, too, Eli. Monster wants me dead, stalker wants you dead."

Tipping her chin up with his knuckle, Eli stared into her eyes. "Which creates the very intriguing question, Sadie. Who is it that wants both of us dead?"

THE QUESTION HAUNTED her throughout the séance.

As if an order had been placed for the occasion, the thunder that had been rumbling over the north woods crept closer. Rain lashed the windows and pummeled the old roof. The raft of candles Molly had lit fluttered atmospherically in a dozen different drafts. Even with Sadie knowing that not a single aspect of this was real, her fingers felt like ice when they joined with those of her tablemates.

Rooney sat in apparent thrall, his eyes closed, his features thrown into skeletal relief by the center candle. Orley seemed annoyed, but surprisingly offered no snotty comments. Brady wore an expression that suggested his mind was elsewhere. Ty looked tense and a little uneasy. Molly might or might not have been in a trance. Jerk jiggled a leg in his chair—out of boredom, Sadie suspected, more than nerves. As for Eli, he watched the entire gathering without appearing to, and occasionally let a small smile cross his lips when her eyes slid to his profile.

Keeping her own eyes firmly closed, Molly attempted to invoke her chosen spirit. "We call to the one who left our world too soon. We seek the knowledge she possesses. We seek truth. We seek—"

The last word was swallowed up by a peal of thunder that made the lids of the teapots rattle.

"You, who were threatened long ago, are dead in body. None among us can say why. But there is one in our realm who knows the truth. One who seeks to repeat his heinous act, who would commit to the afterlife another of your blood. If you can hear me, sister spirit, if you can help us, let your presence and your knowledge be apparent to all. Speak in whatever manner you choose. Send to us a sign that you are among us."

The candles flickered wildly as lightning split the blackness beyond the window. The table bumped. A second later, the door flew open, a blast of cold air rushed in and the candles blew out as one.

It couldn't have been more than two seconds before Eli's flashlight flared. Yet in those seconds, chairs were shoved in all directions and feet clattered. A body—no idea whose—slammed into Sadie, who stumbled into Eli. The flashlight fell and rolled. Ty barked out an order while Jerk—she thought Jerk—grunted.

Eli caught Sadie before she wound up on the floor. "Are you all right?"

"What? Yes. I'm just… Where are we going?"

"We need light."

It took them several seconds to access the wall switch.

By the time the chandelier flared, everyone except Rooney was on his or her feet and scattered.

"Okay." Halfway across the room, Orley raised both hands. "That's it, folks. That was one creepy interlude. I'm not a believer, but I swear, something cold and wet brushed across my face."

"Don't be ridiculous," Ty scoffed. "It was the wind. A shutter blew open in the other room. That blew the door in, and the wind did the rest. Tell her, Eli. Someone's playing a sick prank is all."

"I'd take it a step further and say someone wanted to scare the crap out of us. One of us more than the others, I imagine." En route to the covered furniture, Eli crouched beside his great-grandfather's chair. "You still with us?"

"Didn't spill a drop," the old man replied with a tooth-less smile. He lifted his mug at Sadie. "Pure shinola."

"Sadie?" Molly ventured tremulously.

Willing her heart out of her throat and a calm expression onto her face, Sadie exhaled. "It's fine, Molly. I'm fine. I think Eli and Ty are right. Shutter, door, wet-wind effect, mass palpitations. And yeah, the crap pretty much scared out of us." She regarded Rooney. "It was really good shinola."

Molly's features remained ghost white in the dim over-head light. "I think we can agree that's an ending. Someone or something did not like what we were doing."

"Oh, I wouldn't say that." Sadie glanced at Eli and made a subtle gesture for him to look down. "Someone or some-thing was nice enough to leave me a gift. Not in quite the same condition as the last time I saw it, but I imagine that's the point." Raising her hand, she let Nola's locket dangle on its chain for everyone in the room to see.

The once oval-shaped locket had been smashed so badly out of shape it was barely recognizable. And what she could see that the others couldn't were the two chilling words that had been scored into the old gold backing.

DIE WITCH!

Chapter Sixteen

Yes, she was rattled, but no way would she let it show.

The sight of Nola's locket, which, as far as Sadie knew, had been placed in a safe-deposit box at the local bank two years ago, wouldn't have shocked her or anyone quite so much if it hadn't been hammered flat.

So, not merely struck once or twice with intent to cause damage, but rather bashed to within an inch of its life. Or metaphorically, she supposed, hers.

It took the better part of two hours to search Nola's rooms, clear out the guests and ensure that Rooney was transported safely home. On the way back to the manor, with rain bouncing off the roof of her Land Rover and thunder still rumbling, Sadie turned the ruined locket over in her palm.

"I know this is the monster's handiwork, but why does everything suddenly feel so tragic to me?"

Eli glanced over. "Is that how it feels? I was thinking repressed violence myself. Teetering on the edge of insanity and building for an enraged final act."

"Huh." She regarded the scored words in the next flash of lightning. "You got a lot more out of this particular message than I did. Or maybe than I wanted to. Now, on top of everything else, the killer—monster—whatever—has branded me a witch." She couldn't control the shudder that started in her belly and rose. "Does this mean I'm facing the prospect of eighteenth-century torture tactics, or is it just an incredibly effective way to terrify the living hell out of me?"

"I'd go with the second thing. The witch label's the killer messing with your head."

"In that case, his gamesmanship's bang-on, because I feel totally messed right now."

Eli's next glance held an undercurrent of steel. "Dead's not an option, Sadie, unless your twisted gift giver's playing the part of the corpse."

"He rigged that shutter to blow open and the door after it, didn't he?"

They'd reached a fork in the woods. Braking, Eli reached over and turned her head until their eyes met. "Don't let him do this to you. This is a killer acting out what he can't physically achieve. It's words, and him planting seeds of fear, then hoping they'll take root so you'll do something stupid."

"Like go to a séance in a house full of shadows and draped furniture and really bad lighting. The killer could have shoved a knife in my back as easily as he gave me this locket."

"No." Eli kissed her lightly on the lips. "He really couldn't."

"Trying very hard to believe you here, Lieutenant." She waited through a lightning strike before asking, "Why?"

"Your dress has pockets, right?"

"Yes."

"And you discovered the locket inside one of those pockets."

"Again, yes."

"Did you find it because you felt it being slipped to you?"

"No. I found it when I was helping you look for the light switch, and I bumped into a chair. I felt it—ah, right—on my hip. Got it." The smallest of smiles touched her mouth. "The locket could have been placed in my pocket any time, even before the séance started."

"I'd put my money on before. Were you ever alone in the room?"

"Not really. Molly and I were there together for a while."

"Doing what?"

"Arranging plants and crystals, lighting candles, creating scent zones."

"Did you do a test run with the chandelier off and only the candles lit?

Amusement stirred. "You've met Molly, right? Of course we tested it, several times."

"Were you and Molly alone at that point?"

"By light-testing time? No. Orley, Brady and Ty arrived in a clump. And she paid a couple of delivery guys from the supermarket to bring party trays for after the séance. They came, gawked, placed their trays and left."

"So there were people milling, however briefly. Lights on, lights off, furniture covered, shadows everywhere and you wearing your signature perfume."

"You noticed it?" A smile blossomed. "That's…nice, actually."

His eyes slid down, then up. "There's not much I don't notice about you, Sadie."

Because teasing was easy and fun, she fluttered her lashes at him. "Does this mean we're going to have spectacular sex after all? And before you ask, yes, I've been accused of having a one-track mind before, many times."

"Ditto, but we need to ride out the first track before we switch over. No matter how it was delivered, Nola's locket was intended for you."

"Meaning my monster's target-specific—with lockets, bullets and likely crossbow arrows, as well. Big sigh of relief for anyone who's not me. Or you. Well, sometimes you. I'm confused."

"Actually, you're right on top of it. The killer's not after Rooney or Orley or Jerk."

"Lovely. Again, though, only if you're not me. Or us. Are we done with this conversation, because my brain's about ready to implode?"

"Done enough." He skimmed his thumb over her lips. "For the moment."

Completely off-kilter, Sadie sat back to regard the turbulent night sky while Eli completed the tricky climb to the manor. "You're thinking Cal could have snuck in at the prep stage and given me the locket, aren't you?"

"Ty figures Cal hid under a sheet or behind a piece of furniture while the participants filed in. Séance started, stuff happened, the room went dark and Cal snuck out, nice and tidy."

"Is that what you think?"

"No."

"Gonna tell me why?"

"Are you up for a crash course in police logic?"

"Another 'no' would have done there, Eli." She indicated the far side of the manor. "Park in the carport. If the wind picks up and decides to topple a tree, I don't want it falling on my Land Rover, which still has six months of lease payments left on it."

"You bought this vehicle on a lease?"

Her eyes fired a dangerous warning. "Don't start with me. I know exactly what I gave up to come here and run the *Chronicle. New York Times,* buckets of money, Manhattan condo and monsters who, for the most part, wear business suits." She waited through a long peal of thunder before angling her head at him. "Are you ever going to tell me who it is you almost hurt?"

He parked the Land Rover under the shelter, cut the engine, but left his iPod running. Nirvana might not have been the most romantic of bands, but a driving beat coupled with the screw-you lyrics added an edge to his suddenly closed features.

When he didn't immediately respond, she took a chance and added a gentle "I get that you don't want to talk about it, or her. But if something that happened in your past is preventing us from having amazing sex in the present, can't I at least know part of the reason why?"

Sadie couldn't begin to read his expression when he finally did look at her.

Troubled, angry, brooding, distant. What she could see was his mind sliding back to whatever time had generated those particular emotions.

"Her name was Eve," he revealed at length. "And I came so close to shooting her—killing her—that I blew out a window right behind her."

Whatever horror she'd been anticipating, it wasn't that. Sadie started to speak, reconsidered and sighed. "I don't know what to say, Eli, what I should say. 'I'm glad you didn't shoot her' seems awkward and obvious. But I also know there must have been a reason for that to have happened, and it doesn't involve you falling off some shaky psychological ledge. So let me sidetrack and ask you this. If it was only for one night, and we both knew that, understood and accepted it, could you get around what's been and give yourself permission to enjoy what could be? What is, right now, at this moment?"

Staring out at the night, he gave a small laugh. "You mean can I live, however briefly, in the present rather than the past?"

"Well, yes, but my way sounded much more profound. There's a person out there, Eli, an Ezekiel Blume who wants me dead. If you're Hezekiah and I'm Nola, it makes sense that this modern-day Ezekiel wants you dead, too, before the legend kicks in all the way and you get desperate enough to bring in an evil spirit—and for evil spirit, read backup—to help you trap him."

Traces of that vague humor lingered on his face. "Those recent dreams of yours have really done a number on your head, haven't they?"

"Dreams, bullets, phone calls, text messages, a dead raven, a decimated locket and the knowledge that there are very few places in or out of the Hollow where I actually feel safe."

"I won't—"

"I know. You won't let him hurt me. Kill me. But what if you die trying to save me? Or you die because the monster half of my stalker wants it? I can't think of you dead, Eli. I'm not sure I could live knowing you were gone, whatever the reason." Threads of tension began to creep up her neck and into her skull. "Would leaving Raven's Hollow help either of us at this point?"

"Sadie…"

"Didn't think so. And even if it would, Laura's murderer would still be out there. He'd continue to go unpunished for a crime he committed twenty years ago…. And I have absolutely no idea how we got here from where this conversation started."

"We were talking about me setting aside my emotional baggage long enough for us to make love."

"Interesting how a side trip through hell can put such a huge crimp in such a simple—or I thought simple—question. Forget I asked it, okay?"

"So you don't want to have sex?"

When her temples began to throb, she used her fingers to push back the pain. "I thought I did, but honestly, at this moment? All I want is about six aspirins and a whack on the head to induce sleep. Just walk me inside so I can feed Cocoa, fall into bed and pretend no part of tonight ever happened. You and Ty are clever cops. Join forces and you might actually have this nightmare dealt with before you and or I wind up facedown in Raven's Bog."

She didn't wait for him to open her door, but slid out and set her sights on the entrance.

Painkillers, hot drink, hot bath, bed. It wasn't what she'd thought she wanted, but it would do.

Thankfully, there was no dead raven on the welcome mat, and her front door was locked and bolted. Small favors, major relief. As long as the entry wall was still draped and taped, she'd be fine.

If Eli didn't want to be with her, that was fine, too. No sex, no problem. He wasn't the only person at the manor who had issues. Bellam women sucked when it came to building and maintaining relationships. And she compounded that with a constant need for change. She'd moved from city to city to town so many times over the past seven years that there was very little point in unpacking anymore.

Fortunately, those city stints had taught her how to walk quickly in high heels. She had the door unlocked and opened before Eli made the stoop.

Or thought she did.

One of his hands planted itself on the frame while the other grabbed her arm and spun her around. "Was that your idea of a dramatic exit line?"

He was angry, she realized, and wanted her to feel the same way. No problem. She moved her lips into a sugary smile. "Sorry to disappoint you, Lieutenant, but there was no drama intended. I changed my mind about us, simple as that. Go with the cliché of it being a woman's prerogative. You're not interested, and I'm not willing. Anymore."

She started to turn back, but he held her in place with his body. "You were willing enough a minute ago."

"Well, that's the thing about women in general and Bellam women in particular. We're changeable creatures. One minute we want chocolate, the next it's ice cream. The trick is to catch us before we switch."

His eyes slid down to where he pressed her against the door. "You seem caught from where I'm standing."

"Physically, yes. Unfortunately, I'm not in the mood for chocolate anymore, so back off, Lieutenant, before I call on my ancestor to turn you into that lizard you mentioned once."

His eyes glittered in the next bolt of lightning. "A raven would be more appropriate."

Both her temper and her blood heated up. "Already been done. I'm going for something new. Step back, Eli. Now."

"When we're done here, sweetheart. It's not about me being interested."

It took a second for Sadie to recall her earlier accusation. "If being interested's not part of it, you and I have very different ideas about why people have sex."

"I'm married to my work, Sadie. I have been for the past twelve years."

"Congratulations." She shot him another come-and-go smile. "I hope you make yourself very happy." Exasperation took root. "I said sex, Eli, not a lifetime commitment. I already told you, Bellam women are terrible at forever, so no worries there."

Bracing his other hand on the door, he lowered his head. They were so close now that when the lightning flashed, she saw flecks of gold in his green eyes. "I don't want sex with you, Sadie. I want to make love to you."

"It's the same…." But it wasn't, and her heart recognized the difference instantly. Her mind was another matter. Reining in her annoyance, she sighed. "If that's true, why are we fighting?"

"Probably because I don't want to fall in love with you."

"What? Fall…?" Who said anything about falling in love? Panic scuttled in. "Eli, I'm not… I can't… Did you hear anything I just said? Have been saying all along? Love, marriage, relationships, Bellam women. We're the 'd-y-s' in dysfunctional." She planted her palms flat on his chest. "Most of us never make it to the altar, and those who do make everyone involved wish they hadn't. Ty might not know it, but he's a very lucky man."

"Yeah? So what am I?"

She fisted the T-shirt under his jacket. "About two seconds away from turning ice cream back into chocolate. Eli, understand, this is insanity."

If it was possible, his eyes grew darker. "I'm a direct descendant of Hezekiah Blume, Sadie, remember? Insanity works for me."

Before she could utter another word, he took her mouth with his.

Chapter Seventeen

A dozen objections sprang to mind. Shoving all of them aside, Sadie let her heart—no, not her heart—desire. She let desire take the lead.

Heat scrambled in her veins. Her skin burned. Eli's kiss tortured her senses. And the feel of his body pressed against hers created a ball of lust that gathered in her stomach and then surged upward and out.

Her fingers found his face and held on while he gave and took and ignited. Freeing a hand, she fumbled behind her for the latch—and almost pitched into the manor backward when Eli got to it first.

He caught her easily and swung her around so her spine was plastered to the tall window next to the door.

Every movement spawned a new and exciting sensation. Every touch sparked another flame. Her bones turned to liquid, her thoughts to smoke, her common sense to smoldering ash.

Skimming her curves with fingers and palms, Eli explored her ribs and waist, her hips. Every inch of skin pulsed where he touched. Hunger flared with need trembling close behind it.

She'd wanted this, wanted them to be for so long now it almost seemed surreal. Desperate to taste, she pushed him to the limit, then let him push her back, to the edge and over.

Sadie swore she heard the last threads of protest snap. She'd warned him, and he hadn't listened.

Then again, neither had she.

Playful seduction was one thing. This blind plunge to a place she'd never expected to go stunned her senseless. A small part of her also knew it could and would come back to haunt her.

With the last of her willpower gone, she let the cravings of her body take over. Her head bowed back as she reveled in the shivers that chased themselves over her skin. It was, all of it, magic, a spell whipped up by a mad witch whose mind had been distorted by elemental need.

The air in the manor came alive. Sadie felt the storm swirling around her, into her, through her. She wanted to be closer, to move against him, but her muscles seemed to have deserted her. So she wrapped her arms around his neck and hung on as his mouth returned to feed on hers.

Eli's hands were their own kind of magic. They lit fires everywhere they roamed, and those fires made her energy level swell. As her body grew accustomed to her mind's out-of-control spin, she found herself eager to play catch-up.

Her fingers went in search of his jeans, latched on to button and zipper.

"You want to do this on the entry floor, Sadie?" She heard the faint amusement that lurked below restraint. "Afraid you'll change your mind if we take the time to move?"

She kissed him hard and deep, several times. "Afraid we both will," she said between breaths. "I want this, Eli, more than I've ever wanted anything. It's like—" Her fingers arced through black air. "I'd say it's like flying, except it's more like sinking, and really not caring if you surface or die a happy death and come up smiling when it's over. And since that makes absolutely no sense, why don't we just…?" She finished the question by giving his mouth a nip and bringing the glitter she loved so much to his eyes.

"Yeah, why don't we?" He took the kiss much deeper than she had done. "But not on the floor."

In a finger snap of time, the front hall miraculously transformed into the second-floor landing. She laughed. Crystal night-lights gave off just enough of a glow to guide him along the winding corridor to her bedroom.

Tightening her arms, Sadie caught his earlobe between her teeth and whispered, "Much better than a broomstick, Lieutenant. I never felt my feet leave the floor."

"Glad to hear your mind's not on your feet."

Thunder rumbled through the woods as he set her down in the bedroom. The night-lights dimmed but didn't go out. With need and desire humming, Sadie let him topple her onto the bed. Then her strength returned, and her hunger for him ramped up to critical.

Lightning streaked through the sky. As it did, she wrapped her legs around his hips, tightened and rolled him to a sitting position. "You undid me in the foyer, Lieutenant Blume." Eyes gleaming, she reached for his leather jacket, yanked it off and let it fly. "Now it's my turn."

Holding his arms out to the side, he grinned. "Take your best shot, sweetheart."

"Well, actually—" she got rid of his T-shirt with a quick upward tug "—the shot part's on you. Think of me—" she gave him a push that ended with him on his back "—as your enabler."

She left him his jeans, then sliding from the bed, switched the focus to her. The long slither of black might have been created especially for a striptease. Sadie took full advantage of the design, easing the sleeves along her arms, before running her fingers over her body and up into her hair. Holding it there, she gave her hips a little shimmy until the dress formed a sexy pool of black at her feet.

Stepping out of the fabric, she strolled to where he lay, propped up on his elbows, watching. If her eyes were any judge, he was more than ready to take that shot.

Raising her arms all the way, she allowed her hair to fall and her lips to curve in a deliberate seduction. "Coming to get you, Eli Blume." She crawled onto the bed. "In case you don't know this, a Bellam woman always gets what she wants."

With one very big exception, her heart whispered.

She stopped the whisper before it became a thought and set her mind on the man whose hands were already gliding over her, who flipped her onto her back and under him in a move so smooth she barely noticed it.

Then his mouth came down to plunder, to take everything she could pour into him. The sounds that collected in her throat emerged in a long, low purr. The lightning showed her that his jeans were gone and the only barriers left were her barely there bikinis and a bra that was little more than a whisper of black lace.

When he raised his head, his eyes shone in the slivers of crystal color. A short lightning bolt later, the lace was gone as well, leaving her naked and dazed with the thrill of exposure shooting hungry tremors to all her pulse points.

He had protection and, because of it, her distant but sincere gratitude. A pregnancy, planned or otherwise, was not on the agenda at this point in her life.

Locking his eyes on hers, he bracketed her wrists and drew her arms above her head. She raised her hips to rub against him, a quick tease. He held her there for an endless moment, then uncurled his fingers and ran them lightly down her arms.

His body shifted and lowered. A quick jolt raced through her when his mouth found her breast. He teased the nipple with his teeth and blurred her mind.

Everything around them swirled together in her head. The spears of lightning, white on black, the laser-thin beams of colors, the heat that built so high it threatened to burst through her skin....

She whipped up and over the peak yet still managed to understand that much more waited for her. There'd be another, larger comet tail to grab and ride if she could find the strength to reach for it.

"Now, Eli." Her breath hitched. "Please, now."

She saw him smile. And with thunder shaking both the floor and her bed, he plunged inside her, deep and hard and hot.

Sadie knew she cried his name. Eli simply filled her up. He took her to a place that was both foreign and exquisite. A sensory plane where nothing and everything felt real.

She hovered there for a delicious stretch of time before the ride slowly began to wind down. If the rise had been beyond words, the free fall back was only a little less stunning. A lovely numbness swirled around the edges of her mind and made her want to drift for as long as she could.

Eli was still rock hard inside her, but a deadweight on top. She'd have mentioned it if her tongue had been working. Or her vocal cords. In the end, a hazy "Mmm" was the best she could manage.

"If that was you wanting me to move, not sure I can." Eli spoke the words into her hair. "Not even sure I'm breathing."

"Know the feeling." She set her fingers experimentally on her chest. "Don't think I care." She managed a sleepy smile. "Excellent shot, Lieutenant. I may never walk again."

"I'd say I always aim to please, but you'd probably hit me, and it wouldn't be strictly true anyway."

Keeping her eyes closed, Sadie rode on the ripples of pleasure flowing through her bloodstream. "Spoil my swoony mood, and you're a dead man."

"Not much of a threat all in all. Died about the time I hit peak."

She laughed. "So this really was a one-shot—no pun intended—deal."

"Depends on how good you are at CPR."

The lazy tone of his voice got her juices flowing again, just enough that she wriggled beneath him. "Any chance of a revival happening down there, Lieutenant?"

She heard his smile. "Could be. A little." He raised his head to kiss her. "You said one night, right?"

It took a moment for her thoughts to untangle. "One night of what?"

"Us, Sadie. You said if we only had one night, and we knew it, could we enjoy it without repercussions?"

Unsure whether to be amused or offended, she settled for middle ground and stroked a considering fingernail along his back. "I have to say, you've got a much better postorgasmic memory than I do."

Rising on his elbows, he brushed the hair from her face. "I'm a cop. It's my job."

Offense gained ground. "You do your job in bed?"

His eyes glinted. "I do it everywhere but there, Sadie."

"O…kay." She drew the word out. "That was a fairly decent save. As usual, however, we're sliding off topic. And yes, to the one-night question—though I'm still wondering, in a not entirely nice way, why you asked it."

The glint deepened. "Guess I didn't do my not-cop-related job as well as I thought."

"That being what? To make me forget the who, when and where of tonight's séance?"

He slid his knuckles across her cheek. "For a few hours, anyway."

"In that case…" Her strength restored, she grabbed the duvet and rolled them off the bed. "Storm's still circling the hollow, the night's relatively young and I'm not done with you yet. We did it your way the first time. Now it's my turn." Locking her knees around his hips, she bent forward to whisper, "Wanna bet I can make you forget who, when and what you are?"

"That's a sucker bet, Sadie, but I'm game. Twenty bucks and dinner says not a chance."

She smiled. "Oh, you are so on, Lieutenant." Reaching between them, she stroked him lightly. "Bellam women might not make the best life mates, but we're always up for a challenge." Drawing out a slow kiss, she altered her grip and smiled at his instant response. "I was right about one thing earlier." She kissed him again around his hissed breath of reaction. "This night's gonna be so much fun."

ELI THOUGHT HE'D trained his mind to circumvent any and all nightmares. But with thunderbolts crashing, rain streaming and his senses riding a sexual buzz that made him wonder if someone had slipped him some new and highly illegal street drug, the worst of them returned with a vengeance.

He was in Manhattan, dead tired at the end of a killer double shift. Coupled with the undercover operation he'd completed two days ago, he'd been lucky to remember his own address.

He didn't expect Eve to be there waiting for him, truthfully didn't want her to be. He'd done battle with a lot of demons lately. Junked-up for the most part, but demons all the same. Throwing his own into the mix would simply feed the anger simmering inside him.

Five unrelieved weeks of living in a violent criminal world had scraped his nerves raw. He'd only agreed to the double shift afterward so his partner could be present for the birth of his first child.

Thunder trailed him up a set of dark, endless stairs. His captain said he needed to go under for a while. Threats from the crime boss whose right-hand man Eli had helped expose were the real deal. Anyone, anywhere could have a gun aimed at his back.

Good to know, he thought as he climbed. He was fast and accurate with his own weapons, but if the captain was right and he wanted to live on, he'd need to get faster and even more accurate.

Did he want to live on? he wondered grimly. Or had Eve and her lover sucked his emotions dry?

He'd cared about her, and believed she'd understood. Police officers did not lead normal lives. Her father had been a sergeant in Vice. Between them, hadn't he and Daddy made that simple truth clear? Or had the entertainment magazine she worked for given her a false set of ideals? Yeah, sure, anything was possible—in Hollywood.

He'd gone to her place one night without calling ahead. His mistake, according to her. He'd discovered Eve and her male model lover in bed. Her bed, not his, Eli recalled, which had helped, but hadn't stopped the anger from pushing him into accepting an undercover assignment he hadn't really wanted....

The upper landing of his apartment building took shape at last. Lightning slashed across the East River. He slid his key into the lock, then the dead bolts. Three clicks later, he was inside. Could have hit the light switch, but why bother? He didn't need light to find his bed.

His boots echoed on the worn floorboards. A woman's face flirted on the edges of his mind. Beautiful face, stunning features, incredible smoke-gray eyes....

"Gonna make you forget all the bad stuff, Lieutenant," she crooned. "If Eve had loved you, really loved you, there wouldn't have been another man in her bed...."

Thunder shook the entire building. The foundation bucked and almost threw him into a wall. Okay, got it, totally exhausted.

Then he heard a sound that wasn't thunder, or his boots on the floor, or a sexy female voice turning him on in his head.

Deep inside the shadows, someone moved. So did Eli, simultaneously. He saw a flash of motion, aimed for the torso and only jerked the barrel away at the last second because he spied blond hair.

It was too late to call the bullet back. He swore when the glass shattered, and for a horrible moment thought the shot had gone through flesh before taking out the window.

The woman in the shadow didn't scream. That felt wrong to him. Didn't she always scream in the nightmare? Didn't she scream and run, then stop when shock changed to fury and start throwing things at him?

None of that happened here. Because it didn't, the fear that formed a spiky ball in his belly turned to ice.

He couldn't remember the blond woman's name all of a sudden. Instead, he pictured red-brown hair and features striking enough to make even his great-grandfather's jaw drop.

He froze on that point. Why was Rooney in his head? Why red-brown hair?

The icy ball tightened, shot up into his throat. He saw

her clearly now. Not the woman who should be here, but
Sadie. She stood in front of the shattered window, staring
at him through eyes as dark as the storm. A figure in a
black cloak slunk through the shadows behind her.

Blood gleamed on her left shoulder. Low on her left
shoulder. The figure behind her stopped when he saw that,
and started to laugh. It tossed the knife it held from its right
hand to its left, caught it by the blade.

"Thank you, Lieutenant," it said with a chuckle. "You've
made my task extremely easy."

Muscles bunching, Eli lunged. But in the next lightning
strike, Sadie was gone. Only her blood remained and the
sick, sinking knowledge that he'd killed the only woman
he would ever love.

The eerie chuckle seemed to be everywhere. "So sad,
but that's how it goes for men like us. We who have monsters inside us are what we are. If it will ease the pain of
your loss, however, I give you this balm."

Rearing back, he flung the knife into the center of Eli's
chest.

"Life in hell is deserved, Eli Blume." The voice took
on a weird cadence. "You've forgotten the conjoined legend. Nola didn't die that night in Raven's Hollow. It only
appeared she did. Switch to the present. In this reality, I,
who am Ezekiel, have killed you. You, who are Hezekiah,
will leave this earth before the evil can possess you, while
she, who is Nola—that would be Sadie in case you're getting lost—will be mine. As it always should have been,
Elijah Blume. Sadie will be mine!"

Chapter Eighteen

Eli woke on the bedroom floor, swearing in the unrelieved darkness.

"What?" Sadie rushed in from the hall. Her feet were bare, and she wore a pair of red pajama pants with a white tank. She held a bottle of wine in her hand like a club. "Why did you shout? What's going on?" Her eyes scanned the room. "There's no one here, Eli. Why is no one here if you're shouting? Unless…" She used the base of the bottle to point while he dragged on his jeans. "You had a nightmare, didn't you? The kind that makes you want to turn on every light in the house because it was so damn real."

Crossing to her, he pushed the bottle aside and settled the queasy aftereffects of the dream by kissing her long and deep.

"It was real once," he told her simply, then rested his forehead against hers and breathed in her scent. "I came home under threat after a brutal shift, saw a shadow and pulled my gun on it."

"Except the shadow turned out to be Eve."

"At first, yeah. In my dream it became you, and instead of blasting the window apart, the shot I fired went through your heart. Or seemed to."

She planted the wine bottle in the middle of his chest. "Some people would call that transference, coupled with post-traumatic guilt, bound together with an unabiding sense of frustration. Then and there meets here and now."

"With Ezekiel on a rampage thrown in for good measure." The horror continued to swim in his belly and his brain. "I thought I'd locked the worst of those memories away."

"The subconscious mind's a bitch, isn't it? I do constant battle with mine. Unlike yours, however, mine usually wins, which is why I get headaches, and am not overly fond of going to bed." She kissed the corners of his mouth. "With one stellar exception, plus two on the floor and still plenty of night left as it's only a little after two a.m." Lifting a hand to his face, she softened her tone. "You didn't kill me, Eli, and you and I both know you're not going to. Though I do appreciate the worry."

"The word's panic, Sadie." He motioned at the bottle in her free hand. "Are there glasses to go with that?"

"I dropped them in the hall when you freaked."

"Killed you," he reminded her. "And at worst it was a shout."

"You weren't halfway up the stairs, pal. Cocoa shot past me like she'd been launched from a cannon, and trust me, there's nothing—or very little—that can drag her away from fresh food. However—" she poked his ribs "—if you want to reestablish your manhood, you could light the fireplace for me. I keep it laid and ready. Unfortunately, the chimneys in this house don't draw like they did back in Nola's day."

"You want details, don't you?" Going down on one knee, Eli checked the flue. "It's not a particularly original story."

"Neither was my engagement to Ty. But it was personal, so that makes it important. I'll get the glasses and corkscrew while you ponder and light."

He did ponder, and relive as he stared into the spreading flames. By the time Sadie returned, he had the short version mapped out.

Then tossed it and told her everything, from an interested first meeting through the final night when Eve had thrown a cast-iron skillet at his head.

Afterward, with the fire crackling beneath the sound of heavy rain, Sadie refilled their wineglasses. "I'll give her marks for weaponry, but not for the tawdry affair. Ten bucks says her male model stud was really a wannabe Broadway actor who figured she could use her magazine connections to help him get onstage."

Eli smiled into the excellent burgundy. "I already owe you twenty plus dinner."

"I like Italian, by the way."

"Do what I can."

His eyes strayed from her navel to the swell of her breasts. He knew she was fully aware of his thoughts when she set her glass down and stretched like the cat she'd just fed downstairs. Maybe she was a witch at that. How else could he be rock hard in the time it took to swallow a mouthful of wine?

On her feet and mesmerizing him with every sinuous movement, she reached out to him with both hands. "Don't sweat the—well, I'd say the small stuff, but that's so not true in your case. Leave the past in the past, Eli. This is now." She tugged. "This is us." He stood. "This is hot."

She took the last step between them. Then brought him with her into the fire.

MAYBE THE RAIN would never end. Maybe the thunder would keep him awake. Maybe the monster would develop a conscience and go away. Stay away. Forever.

But he doubted it.

So he was down to pills. Amphetamines. Because he didn't dare fall asleep feeling the way he did.

Sadie didn't want him, would never love him. He understood that now, and the knowledge burned like acid. Not merely in his heart, but in his stomach, in his brain. In the fists he could no longer keep unclenched.

Why did she want Eli, love Eli? Why couldn't she see what was right in front of her eyes?

Because she wasn't looking, that's why. No one ever did, although that was probably for the best. If no one looked, no one saw, and no one would guess the ugly truth.

Anger and jealousy might be the only things saving him from exposure at this point. People bought in to the obvious, shook their heads and felt for the poor rejected soul. Ah, well, they clucked, he'd get over it. Meanwhile, on with life....

He swallowed another pair of pills, rubbed his eyes and tried not to feel bitter. Bitterness was a hot prod in the monster's side.

Why, though, why couldn't he make his fists unclench? Or his teeth? He breathed through them and told himself to let it go. To let her go.

To, please, please, not kill her.

The sound of the rain grew louder. His heart beat faster, his knuckles turned white.

Then, just when he thought his head might explode, someone knocked on the door....

SADIE FIGURED SHE squeezed in two hours of sleep, tops. But she could live with that, because awake, she'd squeezed in, and just plain squeezed, much better things than her sleeping mind could have offered.

Eli was RoboCop, with a cool and sexy twist. He didn't

short out in the shower. They'd gotten wet, had two more bouts of wild sex, then suddenly—morning.

With it had come a grim reality check. What had really happened during last night's séance? Who'd brought the shinola?

Eli wanted answers and after a quick cup of coffee, he rushed her out the door.

Sadie appreciated that he cared so strongly about keeping her alive, but a second cup of coffee and something more substantial than a cereal bar would have been nice. On the upside, the early rush got her to the Hollow just as Molly was stepping out of the pharmacy.

"Eight oh three and all's well. Apparently." She aimed a warning eye at Eli. "Do not destroy my Land Rover."

"Nag, nag, nag." He kissed her twice, then a third time. "Got it. Six months left on the lease. A few more bets like the half dozen you won last night, and it'll be my money covering those payments."

"Never gamble more than you can afford to lose, Lieutenant. Jerk's coming by to stick more duct tape on the printing presses this morning."

"Know it."

"Know you know it. And while we could go back and forth with that one all day, I want to talk to Molly before the eight-fifteen downpour. Vehicle in pristine condition, Eli, or you might find yourself climbing the walls tonight. Literally."

Molly waited for her on the sidewalk. "How can you possibly look so happy after that séance, Sadie? It was horrible."

"I'm picturing a lizard in a black leather jacket—and that séance was staged."

Molly straightened quickly from her slouch. "I didn't set it up. I'm not… Is that what Eli thinks? And Ty?"

"About you, no. About the staging, yes. Eli does anyway. I haven't talked to Ty."

"He came over to my apartment for a few minutes afterward. He was very upset."

"I think we all were."

"All except the person who wants you dead."

"Monster," she corrected. "And I imagine he's beyond upset at this point."

"Ty says it was never actually proven that Cal didn't murder Laura. It was more that the authorities couldn't find sufficient evidence to arrest him."

"I've done the reading, and gone over it with Eli. I know Cal's still a question mark in many people's minds, but why would he want me alive or dead? I'm not sure I even met him as a kid, and as an adult—well, suffice to say, our one and only face-to-face wasn't exactly amiable."

Molly stuffed her hands into the pockets of her smock. "If he's crazy, does it matter why he wants you? For all you know, he might see you as Laura."

"How? There's no physical resemblance between us. Get right down to it, you look more like Laura than I do."

"You're outgoing like she was. You—what's the expression—shoot from the hip."

"Oh, well, now you're talking Orley. She's the straightest shot in the Hollow."

"Maybe Cal's taste in women has changed."

Sadie glanced at the threatening sky. "I really think you're wrong about Cal, but I'm not…"

"He conveniently came into town yesterday, to pick up a prescription for a relative."

"His uncle?"

"If his uncle's Phineas Kilgore, yes."

"So why did he take off when he saw me—us?"

"Sadie, your new beau wears a badge and carries a big gun."

"So does—did Ty."

"You broke off your engagement to Ty. That might have given Cal hope."

"I broke up with Ty in April. It's October now. Cal's had six months to make his move—and don't say he could be a slow mover. Ben Leamer's shown more interest in me since I broke up with Ty than Cal Kilgore has."

"Then Cal has that you know of." Molly emphasized the last four words. "You're perceptive in a lot of ways, Sadie, but not necessarily in the ones that matter, at least not the ones that might make you feel uncomfortable."

The answer stung enough to kindle Sadie's temper, but it was also valid enough that she didn't lose it. Ignoring the first drops of rain, she narrowed her eyes. "What do you mean uncomfortable?"

"You were never going to marry Ty, but you said yes to him anyway. You didn't really love him. Deep inside you knew that, but it took meeting Eli in Boston to pound the truth home."

Guilt coiled in her stomach. "I never meant to hurt Ty."

"I know that, and so does he. It doesn't change the fact that you weren't self-aware enough to know what you wanted or tuned in enough to see that he was totally gone on you."

What Sadie wanted right then was to tell Molly she was wrong, and walk away believing that. But the guilt had a slimy quality to it now, and some of it crawled up into her heart.

She stole another glance at the clouds, then relented. "I'm not saying you're right about all of that, but I did talk to Eli about my—well, choices. Problem is, I didn't go past the words and think about how Ty must have felt when I told him we shouldn't get married."

Molly relaxed her rigid stance. "If it helps, Ty might have been under the same delusion as you. He loved you, and when he thought the future was sealed, he built a fantasy of your life together in his head."

"Then I came back from Boston and blew that fantasy to hell." Which had hurt and disappointed him, Sadie realized, but hadn't resulted in any overt displays of anger until Eli had appeared in the Hollow.

"You look confused." Molly's tone was shrewd, her expression assessing. "I've done my morning prescription check. I came in earlier than usual after no sleep last night. If you want to talk, we can have breakfast at the café."

Because it was unlike Molly to do anything disruptive to her routine, Sadie accepted the offer without thinking.

Maybe she'd been making excuses all her life, she reflected, buying in to a convenient lie. Maybe it wasn't so much that Nola's descendants couldn't commit, but rather that those who chose not to, or failed to do so for the long term, used their heritage as an excuse to walk away. To take the easy and ready-made out rather than deal with life's more difficult problems. And wasn't that an unpleasant conclusion to come to first thing in the morning?

"Sadie?" Molly's voice broke in. "Are you all right?"

"What? Yes...no. I don't know. What time is it?"

"Eight-twelve."

"Okay. We've got three minutes to get to the café, and forty-five after that for you to tell me everything you've noticed about everyone you can think of since Eli came to town. Before that, as well, if it applies."

"I don't know anything about what's happening to you. Or any more than I've already said."

Sadie pulled her down the street toward the café. "We'll talk about Laura, then. You and Orley hung out with her."

"Orley hung out with her." Molly's shoulders hunched. "I was jealous of her." Her eyes rose. "Like I was of you."

"Me? Why?" Frowning, Sadie searched her mind. "When?"

"Well, recently, obviously."

With an absent wave for the counterman, Sadie nudged her cousin out of the incoming flow. "Okay, jealous of me because of Ty, I get. But why jealous of Laura?"

Molly's mouth moved into a tight little smile. "Everyone thinks she was so sweet, but really, Laura was worse than you."

"Me again?"

"Worse than you relationship-wise," Molly clarified.

Completely baffled now, Sadie backed off, hands raised. "All right, I give up. What are you talking about?"

Molly regarded the downpour that had people on the sidewalks running for cover. "Laura wasn't as decent as you were. She didn't break up with Cal until after she found someone else."

"How do you know Laura found someone else?"

"I saw them. Together. In her mother's car. They were making out."

Intrigued, Sadie nudged her farther into the corner. "Did you tell the police?"

"No."

Uh-oh. "Who was she making out with, Molly?"

Her cousin looked her straight in the eye. "You know the answer. You know *because* I didn't say anything." Her lower lip trembled slightly before she firmed it up. "It was Ty."

Chapter Nineteen

Eli had a list of cross-checks in his head and five files open on his cousin's computer when Ty strode into the cramped rear office of the Raven's Hollow Police Station.

"Make yourself at home, Lieutenant."

Absorbed, he switched files. "You okayed this last night, remember?"

"Yes, but I thought you'd at least wait until I came on duty to invade my workspace."

"You were busy with a thing on the other side of…" Eli indicated the monitor. "How secure are the safe-deposit boxes at the bank?"

"Not as secure as they should be if we're talking about Nola Bellam's locket. Molly has the only key. Yes, I asked her where it was, and big surprise, she can't find it."

More comfortable standing than sitting in Ty's office chair, Eli bent over the back of it to open a new folder. "There's a prescription waiting for Cal's uncle at the Raven's Hollow Pharmacy. Order was phoned in yesterday morning."

"Giving him a handy excuse to show up in town yesterday afternoon."

"Handy excuse or legitimate reason."

Ty shrugged out of his rain gear. "My money's on the first thing."

"Why?" Changing folders, Eli looked up. "Come on, Ty, why would Kilgore be stalking Sadie?"

"He forges metal products. Spike strips are metal products."

"He's never sold one to any of the outlets he deals with in Bangor."

"So naturally, never having sold one means he's never made one."

"What it means, if you'd bother to look through his outbuildings, is that Cal makes far more money making moonshine than he does forging metal."

"Which translates to the guy's not a stalker? Sorry, I'm missing the connection."

So was he, Eli reflected and that, together with his cousin's attitude, was starting to piss him off. "One of us should go out to his place."

Ty regarded his cell. "Not sorry to say, Lieutenant, it'll have to be you. Looks like there's some dumb-ass jerk playing chicken with drivers out on the Post Road." For a moment, his scowl appeared to be directed elsewhere. "We all know Kilgore did it. Chief at the time said he'd bet his badge on it. The guy had motive, opportunity and complete crap for an alibi."

"Yeah, I read the report. Mother and grandmother— marginally different stories. The discrepancy wasn't enough to get him arrested."

Pausing in the doorway Ty allowed himself a sneer. "You want the complicated answer, don't you? The one that shows just how good a cop you are."

Eli met his glare. "What I want is the right answer. The one that means Sadie's stalker has been apprehended."

Ty wiggled the fingers of his left hand. "So, no heroics."

Irritation tiptoed through anticipation as Eli pushed

off from the desk. "This isn't about me, Ty, not the way you're thinking."

The fingers of Ty's other hand tightened on the door-frame, but he kept his response level. "If you believe that load of bull, it's more than probable we'll be celebrating two happy events next week. Old Rooney's birthday." He showed his teeth. "And your death."

SADIE'S BRAIN BUZZED for a full hour after she reached the *Chronicle*. In forty-five short minutes, Molly had filled it with more hearsay than she'd have found in a year's worth of newspapers. Most of it had no bearing on her stalker-monster, but the information about Laura could prove useful. All she had to do was separate the things that might connect them in the killer's eyes from those that were merely family ties.

Ty was an obvious connection. However, at different times in their lives, she and Laura had both worked with Brady, organizing large events. In Laura's case, a pair of Cove-Hollow Halloween high school parties. In hers, two charity costume balls.

According to Molly, Laura had also two-timed—or was it three-timed?—Cal with one of the Majerki brothers. Her cousin hadn't been clear as to which brother it was, and possibly it made no difference since Sadie had weekly contact with both men.

Okay, so—candidates for suspicion in place. What next?

After five hair-pulling hours behind her desk, she opted to leave any further business decisions to her PA and headed down to the basement. The ancient presses whirred and clanked and gave new meaning to the term *unholy racket*.

"I could work on these relics for the better part of a year, and they'd still, jam, spit and rattle every time you started them up." Jerk gave the oldest machine a clunk with his oversized wrench. "You should upgrade to newer models."

She patted the press he'd struck. "If I did that, you and Brick would lose your lucrative second income."

"Good point. Are we square about the me-keeping-an-eye-on-you thing?"

"Square enough." She moved toward the archive room. "I'll be breathing in dust until break time, Jerk. Do your best to keep my uncle's babies up and running."

He adjusted his sweat-stained headband. "Your uncle's ancestors, more like. No sneaking out, right, or I could find myself on the wrong end of a witch-hunt."

"A Bellam never sneaks." She grinned. "But you should worry if a raven with red hair flies past you."

The door to the archive room gave an ominous creak as she entered. With its lack of windows, stacks of boxes and general airless atmosphere, it wasn't her favorite place. But this was where the old files and newspapers were stored, and she'd promised Eli to try and dig up a map of the manor grounds.

She started with the back issues that predated Laura's murder by six months. Because the newspapers had been thinner in those days, she was able to go through them, front to back, in a matter of minutes.

Not surprisingly, there was nothing of import prior to her cousin's death. Afterward was another matter—and a more difficult task than she'd anticipated.

Laura had been pretty and smart and fun, and Sadie had loved her. If Molly was to be believed, however, she'd also been busier than most people realized in the dating department. Assuming you could call making out with Ty in the backseat of her mother's car dating.

But so what? So Laura had liked guys. They'd all been hormonal teenagers once, even Molly.

She read the write-ups on the actual murder two times apiece. Nothing unusual jumped out at her. Cal Kilgore remained the number-one suspect in the eyes of most Cove and Hollow dwellers, but the people in charge of the investigation had apparently disagreed. Although he'd been questioned, in the end he'd walked. Out of the spotlight and into the haunted north woods.

While she mulled that over, she unearthed three maps, and one in particular riddled with hidden caves and tunnels that might work for Eli. Speaking of, and given that she'd only caught herself thinking about him twenty or thirty times since entering the room, Sadie felt she was holding her own very well in terms of concentration.

Four months after the fact, the stories surrounding Laura's death began to wane. Other local occurrences took precedence. Some were important and relevant. Many were merely fill.

For instance, in her senior year, Molly had been written up as the girl most likely to become a psychic and open a tearoom in the Hollow. Instead, she'd set her sights on medicine and returned to the Hollow immediately after receiving her degree.

Not to be outdone, Orley had been slated to move to Africa and become the next Jane Goodall. She'd been offered a scholarship to the University of New England, but in the end had chosen to work at the Hollow Veterinary Clinic for three years before heading off to Michigan State.

According to the Blume news feed—that being her uncle's assistant at the time—neither Ty nor Brady had earned anything approaching a scholarship. Brady had fought his way to and eventually through veterinary college, while Ty had hitched a ride to Portland. After eighteen months of bouncing from job to job, he'd finally decided to enlist in the army.

Brick and Jerk had never set foot outside the sister towns—nor been tempted to as far as Sadie could tell.

In Eli's case, the future had been a toss-up. He'd become either a New York state senator or the ultimate pinball wizard. Only Rooney and her uncle's assistant had seen him as a cop, and they'd thought Los Angeles would be his destination of choice.

With her eyes starting to blur, Sadie reboxed the old editions. She hesitated briefly when she spied a headline about a young girl named Lisa Johnson who'd driven her daddy's 1942 pickup through the barrier on Ridge Road in Raven's Cove and been killed on the rocks below. Evidently Laura wasn't the only person in these parts who'd died far too young.

She was hefting the last box onto a high shelf when her cell phone rang. The lack of a name on the screen had her running a palm along the leg of her pants. It took three yoga breaths before she could muster up sufficient courage to answer, "Sadie Bellam."

"Hello, Sadie." The computer-altered voice set her teeth on edge. "You're a very brave woman to go to work under threat of death. Do you have a gun nearby?"

Sidestepping to the door, she looked out. All she could see was the top of Jerk's head, but the sight of him reassured her.

"If you're calling to tell me I'm a dead woman, your threats are getting a little old."

"Don't push me, witch!"

Anger punched through icy fear. "Why? You're pushing me."

"I've also shot at you, with bullets and arrows. It's only Bellam luck that's keeping you alive, and it won't last forever." The rasp dropped to a creepy caress. "I'm an excellent shot."

Sadie scrambled through her memories. Who did she know that was an excellent shot? With guns? Far too many people. With arrows? Eli, Brady, possibly Ty—and every hunter in the area, including, she strongly suspected, Cal Kilgore.

Slipping into the main area, she said, "You made a mistake coming to the séance last night. You've narrowed the field of suspects considerably."

"Only if I let myself be seen. Do you think I did, Sadie? Or is it possible I'm more clever than that?"

When Jerk's head dropped out of sight, Sadie's heart plummeted. But she kept her voice steady and made her way carefully through the presses. "I'll give you clever," she agreed. "But I'm still alive, and that's what counts in the end."

She heard a sudden loud bang above the din, and ducking, raised her eyes to the shadowed rafters.

A low chuckle reached her. "My, you live in a noisy world, Sadie Bellam. But only for a short while longer. Only until you and your cop lover are dead. Then, finally, I'll have what should have been mine from the start."

Still in her crouch, Sadie frowned. "What should have been yours—?"

She had no chance to finish as a deafening explosion rocked the presses and made the floor beneath her tremble.

A second later, the basement went dark.

OUT ON RIDGE Road, Eli finished clamping Rooney's bicycle to the Land Rover's rear rack.

"You know it's five miles to Two Toes Joe's, right? With off-and-on rain and the probability of more thunder and lightning."

The old man made a dismissing motion. "Off-and-on rain's fine, and the *Chronicle* said fog, not another thunderstorm. Weather Channel's only right half the time, grandson. Sadie's closer to ninety percent."

Eli climbed back into the driver's seat. "Still five miles to the Cove," he reminded him. When his phone rang, he read the name and immediately picked up. "Tell me this is a let's-do-coffee call, Sadie."

"If coffee's all you want from me, you must be on speaker with company."

His great-grandfather cackled. "The girl's a regular Miss Marple."

"You think I'm a nosy old woman? That's some compliment, Rooney. In terms of the call, Lieutenant, sharpen your mental pencil. I had another chat with my stalker's nasty side."

Swearing inwardly, Eli looked toward the Hollow. "More of the same, or something new?"

"A little of both, actually." She related the conversation and ended with a sound of frustration. "I'm sure he was going to say more, but one of the presses surged. The motor blew, the electrical panel overloaded and Jerk's eyebrows got singed."

He swore again. "Are you all right? Is he?"

"I'm fine, and you know Jerk. He's already torn the bottom half of the press apart. He says no frigging fossil of a machine's going to get the better of him. Now, before you to do a major burnout in my not-paid-for vehicle, let me add that Brick's already here helping his brother, and I promised Ben Leamer I'd cover a grade-school tour of his corn maze. Personal favor," she added before he could object. "Otherwise, I'd get one of my reporters to do it."

An eager Rooney leaned forward. "Tell Ben I need…" Then he clamped his mouth shut and let a smile lift the corners. "Never mind. Stay safe, young Sadie."

"That shouldn't be difficult in a crowd of more than

sixty." Amusement marked her tone. "Kids love cops, Eli—if you find yourself getting bored in, oh, say, fifteen or twenty minutes."

"I can think of better ways to deflect boredom than by herding a bunch of kids through a maze."

"You were a child once yourself, Lieutenant Blume. That being said, I need to prep for a major headache."

"So basically, you just called to scare the crap out of me."

She laughed. "You said to let you know if anything unusual happened. I think my afternoon qualifies. Oh, and, Rooney? It's as dangerous to ride a bike in the fog as it is during a thunderstorm."

"How can you possibly—?" A sharp burst of static stopped Eli midquestion.

"Hollow Road's not the only place phones tend to pack it in." Rooney shrugged. "She's right, of course, but I like my bike, it's mostly downhill and someone or other's usually driving by if I find myself getting winded." He pointed east. "You heard the lady. Cove's that way, and as you can clearly see, fog's rolling in."

Fine. Great. Sadie had a knack for weather forecasts and a soft spot for Ben Leamer. Eli knew he could live with that. But how much longer would Sadie live if he didn't identify the monster who wanted her dead and bring the bastard down?

"You know," Rooney philosophized, "it'd be better all around if you and Ty worked on this investigation together."

"Still believe in miracles, huh?" Eli glanced in the rearview mirror. "Listen, how'd you like to have dinner with Brady instead of going into the Cove to Two Toes Joe's?"

"I could probably be persuaded—long as he's not neutering something or trying to make me drink that disgusting green liquid he calls tea." Rooney wrinkled his nose. "Gets it from Molly. Supposed to clear the mind, but all it did was put me to sleep. A stiff shot of Ben's..." He glanced sideways. "Let's just say my special tonic does the job much better." He thumped his cane. "Now, talk to me, grandson, about this man who's haranguing our Sadie."

"He's not haranguing her." Eli squinted at a truck several hundred yards ahead. "He's trying to kill her. Or half of him is."

"That'll be the Ezekiel half."

A wry smile formed. "You don't miss much, do you?"

"Sure didn't miss the expression on your face when you talked to Sadie."

"Would that be the expression of abject fear or ball-crushing fury?"

"Some of both, I expect, mixed with what I'm betting was a night of mutual satisfaction and multiple org—"

Eli cut him off with a look. "Finish that thought, and I'll strap you to the rack with your bike."

His great-grandfather made a scoffing sound. "Does Sadie know you're a prude when it comes to discussing sexual relations?"

"She's a woman, Rooney. No conversation's taboo. You're welcome to have this one with her and leave me with the simpler task of keeping her alive." He spaced out the last three words for effect and at the same time managed to get a clear enough look at the truck ahead that his adrenaline began to pump. "Oh, yeah. Time you and I had another chat, pal."

Rooney snorted. "Chats with prudes bore me."

"Not you and me." Eli nodded forward. "Me and him. That's Cal Kilgore's truck."

"Well, hell, in that case, put the pedal down, and we'll head him off at the pass."

"What pass?"

"Hang a left at the crippled oak, and I'll show you." He flapped a blue-veined hand. "Left, left."

With curses rolling off his tongue, Eli made the turn. At Rooney's urging, he bumped along a rough path, down a hill, through a river of mud and into a stand of trees that came within an inch of scraping the paint off both sides of Sadie's vehicle.

"There, you see?" his great-grandfather crowed. "Road."

But not before dip, crevice, pothole, pothole, pothole. Eli had a quick vision of himself as a lizard, then miraculously the pathway opened up and he was back on the main road. He saw Cal's truck barreling toward them, swung into a hard one-eighty and, slamming on the brakes, successfully blocked both lanes.

There was no mistaking the blind panic on Cal's face as he executed a squealing quarter turn. The maneuver put the two men door to door with less than eighteen inches of misty air between them. While Eli squeezed out, gun drawn, Cal scrambled across the passenger seat and into the gully.

There was nothing Eli relished more than a chase, and Kilgore was agile enough to give him a good one. If he had a weapon, he didn't use it. Or he'd left it behind.

The minute he skidded into the hollow, Cal ditched the path and started to weave—through the trees, around a murky pond and over a pair of questionable bridges. With Eli gaining, he splashed through puddles, used logs as launching pads, and finally made the mistake of trying to cross Raven's Creek on a scattering of crooked stones.

Tucking his gun, Eli bypassed the stones, took aim at his ankles and went for a low tackle.

A muffled "Oomph" preceded a sharp back kick and

a twist that almost allowed Cal to kick him in the face. Eli just managed to get a forearm up to deflect the blow.

"Bastard," Cal spat.

"Took the words," Eli muttered, then rolled sideways as his quarry's scrabbling fingers got hold of a stubby branch.

He swung it hard, but another roll took Eli out of range and probably sent pain singing up Cal's arm when he struck a tree.

Eyes watchful, Eli redrew his gun. He didn't aim, merely held it up and off to the side while he gauged Cal's labored body language. His wet clothes appeared to be weighing him down to the point of exhaustion.

"Are we done?" he shouted.

On his hands and knees, Cal brought his head up. A snarl formed. He pounded the water with his fists.

"We'll call that a no."

When the other man flew toward him, Eli bounced to the right, used his elbow, his foot and his fist, in that order.

The guy had a granite jaw, but a poor stance in the stony creek bed. The punch he attempted to land resulted in a yelp as he lost his balance and flopped onto his stomach in the water.

"That works." Stuffing his gun in his waistband, Eli planted a knee in Cal's lower back, grabbed a handful of his hair and gave it a deliberate yank. "Talk," he ordered, "or I'll turn you over and make a eunuch out of you."

Cal locked his good eye on Eli's face. "You're too well trained to hurt a prisoner."

"Don't count on it. I'm in a pisser of a mood right now."

A long glare preceded a hiss of breath. "I'd say bull, except there's a woman involved, so you might just follow through. If this was about a guy…"

"It is about a guy." Eli wrenched him none too gently

onto his back and set a warning knee on his thigh. "It's about a stalker with a homicidal id."

Cal's other eye circled wildly. "You're not a shrink and I'm not a murderer. We went through all this when you showed up on my property unannounced."

"We went through some of it," Eli agreed. "Things have happened since. Why did you take off yesterday when Sadie noticed your truck?"

"You can't guess?"

"You hate cops."

"Damn straight. Every one I've known has tried to pin Laura's death on me."

"And you think running's going to change that?"

"I didn't run until you and your tight-ass cousin came after me."

Shifting his knee, Eli pressed a little harder on Cal's thigh. "People who run usually have something to hide. What're you hiding, Kilgore?"

"Not a secret yen for your lady, if that's what you're thinking." He sucked air through his teeth when Eli shifted his knee again. "You hurt me, Blume, and I'll sue. I've got rights."

"What you've got," Eli corrected, "is about five seconds to start talking."

"You're out of your jurisdiction."

"Two seconds."

Cal uttered a single rude word. "All right, you win, upper hand. I came to get some pills for my uncle."

"Figured that much. Why take off yesterday?"

Cal swung his good eye to the side, gave a mirthless laugh and closed both. "You won't believe me."

"Stalling's not your best bet here."

"I'm not stalling. The brown truck gave me heebies."

"Brown truck," Eli repeated. "Brady's truck?"

"I saw him get into it maybe an hour before Sadie spotted me in town. Only this wasn't your average man in the woods. This guy was wearing a long black cloak with a big, floppy hood. So floppy you couldn't see his face."

"Go on," Eli said when he paused.

"He was moving fast. He opened the door of the truck, tossed a mother of a gun inside and took off. I didn't know if he'd seen me or not, so I stayed put until I was sure he was gone."

"Where were you, Cal? Exactly."

"Partway up the hill that leads to Bellam Manor."

"Yeah? Why is that?"

"I was waiting for someone. Look, d'you want this or not?"

Did he? Slick knots twisted in Eli's stomach, but he loosened his grip and sat back. "Go on, finish it."

"From the look on your face, I don't have to." Cal regarded him half-lidded. "My eyes only act wonky, Lieutenant. They see fine. The guy pushed his hood back when he drove off. Then he turned his head just far enough that I got a real good look at his face."

Something like dread slithered into Eli's chest, but his gaze didn't falter. "I said finish it."

"It was your cousin in that truck. Your cousin, wearing a big black cloak and carrying a badass gun. That's why I ran. He was standing next to that brown truck when I stopped at the intersection in town. He looked up when he saw me, looked right straight at me, and I'm telling you, my guts turned to water. I'll tell you something else, too. Thinking back like I have been since that happened, I realize yesterday's not the first time I've looked at his eyes and felt that way."

Because no part of him wanted to hear this, Eli snagged another handful of Cal's jacket and yanked him up. "Are you telling me my cousin Brady shot at Sadie and me in the woods near Bellam Manor?"

Cal's eyeball swam in its loose socket. "I'm saying I saw a guy in a cloak get into a brown truck. But yeah, it could be I'm saying he used that gun on you, because I heard shots a few minutes before he came crashing out of the old tunnel."

The last two words only registered on the fringe of Eli's mind. Right then, all he could see was Sadie's face. And behind it, like an evil black cloud, his cousin Brady's.

Brady, who'd taken the time to text her as he drove away. Brady, who'd told her he hadn't been shooting at her. Because Brady was only obsessed with her.

It was the monster that wanted her dead.

Chapter Twenty

Sadie planned to leave the newspaper immediately after talking to Eli. Unfortunately, as she was pulling on her leather coat, another printing press decided to go down—and take two-thirds of the *Chronicle*'s power with it.

When she reached the basement, Jerk muttered something about never having eyebrows again. Then he bared his teeth, stripped off his shirt and dived headfirst into the wires.

It was closing in on six when she finally jogged across the parking lot to the ancient Bronco her copy editor had—maybe kindly, maybe not—offered to lend her.

She called Ben as she went, half hoping he'd tell her not to come, but it seemed the school buses hadn't arrived on time, either, so everyone was running late.

The Bronco was so old and worn she couldn't even use her rusty standard-shift driving skills as an excuse to cancel. The engine ground a bit but slid obligingly from gear to gear whether she engaged the clutch properly or not.

So—plenty of time to think about Eli, the night they'd spent together and how the hell she was going to deal with the fact that her heart did a tap dance whenever his face popped into her head—which was every other minute at this point.

The big question had been rearing its head all day. Did

she love him? To her dismay, the big answer scared her as much as it thrilled her.

How could a relationship between them work? Did he even want a relationship? Did she?

Love, she reminded herself, was supposed to make overcoming obstacles not only possible but also enjoyable. Of course, in their case she had to factor in a strong fear of commitment on both sides, a near tragedy on Eli's and a massive failure on hers. All in all, their obstacles read more like mountains, and that was before she compounded them with the grisly fact that someone who had two distinct personalities appeared to want both of them dead.

It might be a formidable weapon, but even love couldn't deflect bullets or arrows. Meaning, for the moment at least, she needed to set her feelings aside and focus on staying alive to pursue them.

She eased up on the gas as she drove past the police station. Maybe she should have told Jerk she was leaving. If nothing else, she'd have had peace of mind knowing he was tailing her.

But the presses had to be repaired, and no one except Jerk would be stubborn enough to make that happen.

As she drove past the police station, she noticed that Ty's cruiser was gone, and both the veterinary clinic and the pharmacy had closed an hour ago.

No lights burned either in Brady's apartment or in Orley's. Or none that she could see through the layers of fog that were thickening as she drove.

Would Eli really attempt to track a monster in this stuff? Was it possible that he and Ty had joined forces?

Well, yeah, about as possible as the prospect of her stalker packing up and moving to Florida.

Pressing on a temple that had been threatening to throb all day, Sadie concentrated on the road. More correctly, she concentrated on the two feet of road she could see with her eyes and not her memory.

The passing minutes stretched into forever. Even with Van Halen and David Lee rocking it out, her hands were damp on the steering wheel. It wasn't until she realized that her fingers were strangling it that exasperation took over and had her growling, "Enough!"

One resolved breath in and out relaxed her shoulder muscles. For a moment. Then the tension knots doubled as something—no, someone—took shape directly ahead.

Clenching her teeth, Sadie braked hard and stared at the haloed person for three disbelieving seconds. Then her trance broke, the jagged edges of fear gave way to spikes of temper and she kicked the Bronco's slightly dented door open.

"Are you insane?" she demanded, striding forward. "I could've killed you."

Her cousin Orley scooped the fingers of both hands through her hair. "Start with me, Sadie, and that's exactly what I'll do to you. I picked up a nail—left rear tire. It's the third puncture I've had in six months on this ridiculous excuse for a road."

Still steaming, Sadie went toe-to-toe with her. "Why, unless you're suicidal, are you standing in the middle of this ridiculous excuse for a road?"

"In a word? Favor. In a name? Ben Leamer." She rapped the sides of her head. "You'd think I'd learn, wouldn't you?"

"What? Not to do favors, or not to stand on foggy roads?"

"Both, apparently. And to carry a spare tire that doesn't have a frigging hole in it." When Sadie's lips quirked, a warning finger came up. "Laugh and I'll toss you into the hollow, take your—whatever that thing is you're driving—and leave you stranded." She gestured from herself to Sadie. "Black belt, no belt."

"Been a lot of years since you earned that black belt, Orley." Tipping her head from side to side, Sadie said, "If you want a ride, you'll have to follow through and come to the farm with me. I don't think my copy editor's spare will work on your Jeep."

"As we appear to be the only live humans on this god-forsaken road, offer accepted. Here, take my flashlight. I'll get the rest of my…" Trailing off, she peered past Sadie into the swirling fog. "Do you hear something?"

"Other than the receding sound of my heartbeat, no." But she turned to listen.

"I know that engine. Do I know that engine?" Brow knit, Orley strained to see. "Whoever it is, he's coming fast."

Sadie gave her a nudge, then a push. "He's coming fast, and he's not slowing down."

"That's Brady's truck, I'm sure of it."

"Then Brady must be drunk."

Sadie tried to gauge his wild approach so they wouldn't actually have to jump into the ditch to avoid him. She was on the verge of diving in when he screeched to a halt ten feet ahead.

After several noisy attempts, the driver's door crashed opened and Brady tumbled out. He leaned heavily against the side. "Don't die! Please, don't die!"

"Wasn't planning to," she murmured, then raised her voice. "Why are you here, Brady?"

"Monster." His head snapped up. "Gonna kill you."

Sadie swore. "Move," she said to Orley.

"What? Where? Wait a minute, what am I saying? It's Brady."

"Who just said the monster's going to kill me." She

dug out her phone. "Why do I know this thing's not going to work?"

Bracing his hands on his thighs, Brady shouted, "Get away. You have to get away!"

"It must be drugs," Orley whispered. "Mixed prescriptions maybe. He looks really zonked."

Eyes widening, Sadie snapped the phone from her ear. "He's got a gun!"

The hand holding it shook as Brady straightened. "Run, Sadie." He looked straight at her. "Run from the monster!"

Orley eased behind her. "Please say your phone has a signal."

Sadie shook her head, watched Brady's trembling right hand. "We need to go. Now."

"But there's only the hollow. Nowhere else, only there."

Weapon arm raised, Brady took aim.

"Run!" Sadie shoved her cousin toward the ravine. "Climb down or slide, it doesn't matter which."

Brady's mouth stretched into a horrible grimace. "Gonna kill you, Sadie. Get away!"

Luckily, he caught his foot and stumbled sideways. The gun went off. Into the air, Sadie hoped as she followed Orley over the edge of the road and onto the treacherous slope that dropped more than a hundred feet into the hollow.

Stopping on a ledge halfway down, Orley muttered, "This is not happening."

Sadie gestured with the flashlight. "Go right. It's less of an obstacle course." But she ran into two rocks and wound up skidding on her butt even so.

Didn't matter. Brady was right behind them. She could hear him breaking small branches and dislodging stones as he mimicked their descent.

Momentum would have flung her into a tree at the

bottom if she hadn't slammed feet-first into a huge exposed root.

A short distance away, Orley groaned. "Are you alive? Am I?"

"I'm here." Unwilling to use her flashlight, Sadie found her more by feel than sight. "We need to keep moving."

Nodding, Orley climbed to her feet.

The fog in the hollow varied from thick and swirling to layers of gauze. In an odd moment of clarity, Sadie saw the moon raining thin beams of silver through the mist.

It wasn't her nightmare, not exactly, but it felt close. Something evil chased her through the woods. Instead of a knife, however, all she had was her cell phone—and no signal!

"I'm not the monster!" Brady's echoing shout reached them from several yards back.

"He's sounding fuzzier by the minute," Orley gasped from behind. "We could ambush him. Not hurt him, but— you know—quick bop on the head, send him under."

Halting, Sadie drew in much-needed air. "Incapacitate Brady, incapacitate the monster."

Orley cast an uncertain look around. "Right. How do we make that happen?"

"I'll get his attention." She steeled herself. "You'll have to hit him." As the thrashing came closer, she shone Orley's flashlight on the ground. "We need a branch."

They found one stuck in the mud and yanked it free.

"Ready?" Her cousin took up a stance, arms over her head and poised to strike.

Sadie had no chance to reply as Brady burst out of the fog.

He slowed when he saw her. His face crumpled. "I'm not the monster," he promised. "I don't think I ever—"

Darting into a wash of moonlight, Orley brought the branch down on his head.

Brady went rigid. He staggered a step, let the gun slip from his fingers. Then, just as Ezekiel had done in her nightmare, his eyes rolled back and he dropped to the ground at Sadie's feet.

FOR THE FIRST time in his life, Eli knew what it would be like to live in slow motion. Every second was an agony. Only his mind raced, and the thoughts it spawned shot through so fast he couldn't catch most of them.

He hauled Cal back to the Land Rover—no idea how or what kind of time that took—then headed for the Hollow, another underwater slog. More terrifying than anything, however, was the fact that he couldn't get hold of Sadie, either at the *Chronicle* or on her cell phone. What he did discover was that Jerk hadn't gone with her.

It felt as if hours passed before the lights of Main Street appeared. Reaching over, Eli braced Rooney for a squealing stop outside the police station. He only glanced briefly at Cal, who sat in mutinous silence in the backseat, cuffed to the door.

"Get Ty or one of the deputies," he told his great-grandfather. "I'm going up to Brady's apartment."

His cousin's truck was gone, he noted as he ran. No lights burned upstairs, the clinic was dark—and Sadie was driving to Ben Leamer's farm in the fog. Alone.

He climbed the stairs two at a time and didn't bother to knock, just booted the door open and led with his gun. Using his elbow on the light switch, he let his mind spin through the possibilities as his eyes searched the room.

Cal insisted he'd seen Brady coming out of the woods yesterday afternoon. But was that a true account provided by a witness or a desperate lie concocted by a murderer?

Eli crossed the floor with caution, because he knew, somehow knew, Cal hadn't been lying.

A teapot sat on the dining table. A hard-backed chair lay on the floor. He spotted a single black mug, three-quarters full. The contents were warm but not hot.

Rescanning the room, he speed-dialed Sadie's cell. And ground his teeth when the call failed. He tried Brady with the same result.

He was checking out the teapot when his phone vibrated. "Brady's the stalker," he said to Ty on the other end. "Sadie's on her way to Ben Leamer's farm. I called Ben and told him to send his hired hand to meet her on the Hollow Road."

A confused "What?" was the best Ty could manage. "What?"

"I'm in Brady's apartment. There's powder residue on the lid of the teapot. Could be PCP."

"What?" Ty demanded again. "You think Brady's doing drugs? And that he wants Sadie dead?"

"You need to meet me on the Hollow Road."

"I can't. Not quickly. I'm miles from there, all the way out on Spirit Point. There was a call. Three-car collision. Except…"

"There was no collision."

There was something, though. Eli could feel it. Some not-quite-right detail that held him in Brady's apartment when he should have been breaknecking it for the hollow. Some twisted truth that needed to be unearthed.

A photo album covered with cartoon animals lay on the floor under the table. With Sadie's face flashing in his head, he crouched to flip it open.

Some not-quite-right detail…. Something he needed to know before he went after Brady….

The pictures glared up at him. Hell, they all but sprouted

fingers and grabbed him by the throat. Shot after shot, page after page, year after year, in a sick and steady progression that chronicled the life of Brady Blume.

And the monster who wanted Sadie dead.

"DON'T GET TOO close to him, Orley." On her knees, Sadie searched the ground for Brady's gun.

"It's here. I've got it." Orley squatted near his head. "Don't worry, he won't be waking up any time soon. Between the whack I gave him and the cat tranqs, he'll sleep for at least four or five hours."

"Four or five…?" Something in her cousin's tone sent a wintery chill through Sadie's bloodstream. She flattened her palms on the ground and without looking up forced a calm "What cat tranqs, Orley?"

"I put them in his tea. I always put them in his tea or coffee when I need him to be good and sleep for me."

Sadie's heart began to thud. "Sleep," she repeated carefully. "For you."

The gun came into view first, followed by the hazy oval that was Orley's face as she smiled over Brady's prone body.

"Surprise." She spoke softly and with no small amount of malice. "Aw… you thought Brady came here tonight so the monster inside him could do its nasty worst, didn't you? Well, take heart, cousin, I daresay he thought the same thing. Although—hard to say, maybe not. Oh, there's a monster, but it doesn't live in Brady. It lives, Sadie dearest, in me." Her smile widened. "It's green and it's mean and it's sick to death of not getting what—or rather who— it wants. Who it's wanted since before it made Laura a corpse and left her in the slime pool we call Raven's Bog."

Astonishment simply robbed Sadie of thought. "You're not serious," she managed. Yet even through a curtain of shock, Orley's gleaming eyes told her she was. Serious and deadly. She'd murdered their cousin Laura twenty years ago.

And would, without qualm or hesitation, murder another of her cousins tonight.

Chapter Twenty-One

Waving the gun like a pennant, Orley forced Sadie to stand. "I can't say I'm impressed. You're supposed to be a crack journalist, someone who sees what others miss. How did you miss what's inside me?"

It amazed Sadie that her temper would rise with her fear. "You weren't a story to be dissected and probed. You were just my cousin with an attitude."

"And a gun."

Wisdom elbowed temper aside. "And that." Although she couldn't see it succeeding, she went with a rational approach. "Oh, come on, Orley, why would I think you had a monster inside you? We're family. I've always seen you as one of the most stable people I know. I think of us as friendly rivals."

"Excellent. Shot to the heart. Applause, applause. Won't work, of course, but marks for effort. See, here's the thing. While I do in fact like you much better than Laura, I don't like you enough to let the man I've wanted—since I was five years old—" she enunciated the last six words "—destroy his life and my dreams, which I swear are going to come true as soon as you're gone. Brady thinks he has an alter ego. He believes that alter ego is murderous. But like most of us, he doesn't relish the prospect of spending the rest of his life behind bars. So—self-preservation mode."

Sadie heard her through an ever-increasing shriek of denial. Orley had killed Laura two decades ago when they were seventeen. Killed her because Brady had wanted her. Really? Seriously?

"This is sick, Orley. This is totally sick."

"This is necessary."

An incredulous laugh emerged. "You think making Brady believe he has a monster inside him is necessary? You think that's love?"

"Don't psychoanalyze me, Sadie. Brady's the one who decided he had a slice of Hezekiah Blume in his soul, not me. I just went with it."

"Why? Because it worked for you?"

"Yes. And the only thing I'll say in my defense is that it's not what I had in mind the first time I drugged him."

She adjusted her grip on the gun she held—in her left hand! The irony of that observation struck a note of absurd humor and had Sadie closing her eyes for a moment.

"Ah, there. You see it now, don't you? But give yourself a break, cousin. You weren't looking for a left-handed woman. Surprise again." Orley's smile stretched wider. "I worried about the chop to Laura's skull after I'd done it. Then it occurred to me. Given the phone calls she'd surely have mentioned to someone, and the obsessive notes that would undoubtedly turn up at some point, no one would be thinking 'female killer.' Plus, there was Cal. So I relaxed, played the sorrow game and kept a close eye on Brady."

Impossible images swam in Sadie's head. "You found out that Brady wanted Laura, so you murdered her. Simple as that."

"Murdered her after she broke up with Cal." Crouching, Orley set her fingers on the pulse point in Brady's neck. "Until then, she was unattainable. I could deal with that. Dumping Cal was her fatal mistake. Brady started thinking he could have her, and—well, that wasn't going to happen. So—desperate-measures time."

"You worked at the veterinary clinic in high school." Sadie forced herself not to look at the gun, not to appear to be looking at anything while her mind raced. "You had access to sedatives and anesthetic."

"The doc at the time didn't keep accurate supply records. Neither did his assistant. All brilliant me had to do was read and learn and come up with a dosage that would work on humans."

"A dosage of what?"

"Ketamine. Street name, cat tranqs. It causes all sorts of nasty problems—hallucinations, confusion, agitation and, of course, unconsciousness. I slipped it to Brady from time to time, hoping I could scare Laura into leaving town. I tacked on a threat to a larger-than-life love note Brady gave her. Just intercepted it before she was aware and turned Brady's love note into a monster's portent of doom."

"That's why the writing changed," Sadie murmured.

"That's why. Didn't have the desired effect, of course. Laura's senior year loomed, and she had a brand-new family that she liked. All I had left was death."

"Right. Death. With no second thoughts. No remorse. Nothing."

Orley leaned in to stage-whisper, "We weren't friends, Sadie, only unfortunate relations. I never liked her, or Molly—or people in general for that matter. In your case, all was well enough while you were engaged to Ty. Oh, Brady saw and Brady wanted, but lucky you, Ty got there first. A long courtship blossomed into an engagement. Then, uh-oh, wedding in Boston. Chance meeting with Eli. Next thing I knew, Ty was unengaged, and Brady's hopes were soaring. Damn. Time to start plotting again. Here's the kicker, though, cousin. Who should appear on the very day that Brady worked up the nerve to make an anonymous phone call to your office but Eli Blume?"

Sadie struggled to keep up. "Are you saying Brady sent me that animated e-card?"

"Yep. It was his way of testing the water. Far as I can tell, the dead raven on the doorstep was more of a gift gone wrong. He meant to leave a live raven in a gilded cage. But the raven got loose and flew up into the porch rafters. Brady tried to flush it out with a gunshot—and, well, I guess the bird wasn't where he thought, and it plopped down dead at his feet."

"Why did he leave it there?"

"I imagine killing it rattled him. Plus, he still had a message to write. So in he went, home you came and uh-oh, gotta run. If my deductions are correct, and I'm sure they are, he 'borrowed' one of Ben Leamer's old trucks for the occasion. You know Ben. He's got a barn full of the things. Talk about your perfect setup. FYI, the call Brady made to you that day was his last. I used the same freaky computer voice to do the rest."

Sadie stared. "How do you know all this?"

"I get him to talk. After I drug him and before he goes under, I grill him. Sometimes he slips away before I get everything, but mostly I can eke out the details. I'm a very clever Bellam, Sadie. And Brady's mind has always been wonderfully malleable."

"Is that what you call it?"

"You think he's unbalanced, don't you?"

"I don't know what I think at this point. Maybe unbalanced. Or maybe confused—because he thinks he's got a homicidal maniac living inside him!"

"Don't take that tone with me," Orley warned. "Remember who's holding the gun here. Any imbalance in Brady's personality is a result of him being totally repressed. Fortunately, I haven't got a repressed bone in my body."

"Okay, wait." Hands raised, Sadie took a step back, both physically and mentally. "Backtracking here. You're telling me that, being repressed, Brady had to resort to weird tricks to get my attention, whereas you, who aren't the slightest bit repressed, have no problem approaching anyone."

"I'm way ahead of you, Sadie. You're wondering why I didn't just let Brady know I wanted him instead of going all extreme killer."

Anger seeped through terror. "It would have been a saner option. Not to mention kinder, and—brass tacks here—less of a risk to your own—" she almost said "stupid" but swallowed that and left it at "—life."

Closing the gap between them, her cousin tapped Brady's gun to Sadie's chest. "You see, now, that's why I like you so much better than Laura. You're mere seconds away from death, and here you stand, totally pissed off at me for not telling Brady how I felt about him."

"Thereby avoiding the 'seconds away from death' part," Sadie said through her teeth.

Orley's features hardened, and this time when the gun struck Sadie's collarbone it stayed put. "I did tell him, in every way I could think of. I even lowered my career goals so I could be his assistant. I tried to seduce him at high school dances, went for it again at college and twice more after we came back to the Hollow. Every damn time I came on to him, he got awkward and flustered and insisted we were friends. Best friends but—and this part was strictly between the lines—friends without benefits."

He hadn't wanted her. A very small part of Sadie actually felt sorry for her.

Orley shook back her hair. "Didn't matter what he said, what he felt then or what he thinks he feels now. He'll be mine after tonight, I'll make sure of it. Just know this. He wanted you more than he wanted Laura, and I still did everything I could not to kill you. For some reason, he refused to be deterred by Eli. Guess he got tired of backing down. He wanted you to be his and Eli to be gone."

"Are you saying it was Brady who tried to kill Eli?"

"Hell, yes. And while my intention at first was simply to be rid of you, that plan changed when I realized what Brady was prepared to do to get you. I knew he'd bungle the whole thing and wind up in prison, so I decided to do it all. I'd kill Eli for him and you for me. Problem solved— at long, long last."

"Who shot the crossbow arrows at us?"

"Oh, come on. My father's a hunter. I'll admit I hate that about him, but he insisted on teaching me how to handle a crossbow. I told you, my original goal was to frighten you into leaving the Hollow. Eli, too, if possible. The love thing was obvious, so I figured if you left together, the monster could go back into hiding."

"When did it all become real for you?"

"When Brady went after Eli near Bellam Manor. The bullets he shot were meant to kill. I used the concerned citizen call about the injured deer to cover for him, when in fact I dealt with the problem all by my lonesome."

Sadie stared. "Is this really happening?"

"Talking here, Sadie," Orley warned. "Brady didn't show up until I was almost finished. And I didn't know what he'd done on the manor grounds until I spotted the cloak and gun in his truck. I talked to you a little while later, but it wasn't much of a leap from the cloak and gun alone, given his rattled condition and my intuitive nature. I gave him the crossbow from the deer—call it a prop—

got him to help me clean up the mess and off we went in our separate vehicles, back to the Hollow."

"You make it sound like an average day at work."

"Hardly average. I still had a séance to rig, and a locket to steal and decimate. The last two things were easy enough, but my fingers were crossed big-time during the séance. Storm helped, and we all know how old the manor's window latches are. To be honest, I wasn't sure every last candle would blow out when the window burst open, but what do you know, they did. I took it as a sign that I was meant to succeed."

"Yes, you're a lucky monster, aren't you? Still, you know as well as I do that nothing, not even luck, lasts forever."

"Shut up, Sadie. This conversation is over. I'm going to kill you and Eli and give Brady an airtight alibi for the time of the murder. Ty's off on a phony emergency call, and sooner or later, Eli will come looking for you. He'll see your body, rush in and whack, whack, end of problem."

Keep her talking, Sadie's instincts whispered. She took a cautious step back. "What about your car?"

"It's well hidden. Unfortunately, Brady's truck isn't, so—time we moved this party along."

Panic spurted through Sadie's veins. "It won't work, Orley. You got lucky with Laura. This is far more complicated." At Orley's fierce look, she gestured behind her. "You can't carry Brady out of here."

"I'll hide him and his truck. Convince him to let me handle everything once it's over."

"And let him go right on thinking he's a monster."

"It'll keep him in line and indebted to me. One lovely side effect of ketamine is that when a person wakes up after ingesting it, he or she has no recollection of what transpired. Brady invented the monster, Sadie, not me.

Remember that. And stop backing away. One step more or less won't make you a smaller target."

Sadie edged sideways instead. The ground was growing increasingly slippery as it began its descent to the murky water of the bog.

"They'll trace the gun, Orley."

"Well, duh." One of her cousin's feet slipped, but she seemed not to notice and wagged the barrel instead. "This is a .45, if you don't know weapons. It belongs to Ben Leamer. I lifted it the day we met Hezekiah's effigy in the corn maze. Let me tell you, that message you got about not waking the monster came as quite a shock to me."

Sadie fought to hold her balance in the mud. "I'm sure I'll sound obvious, but if you really loved Brady, you wouldn't be doing this."

"If I did nothing, I'd be Molly." She raised the gun. "Time to die, cou—"

As Sadie had hoped, the slippery ground took Orley's feet out from under her. She landed on her hip and lost her grip on the gun.

The instant she fell, Sadie bolted. Away from the bog and into the heart of the fog-shrouded woods.

She didn't know if Orley was behind her or not. She only knew this was very much her nightmare. A deadly pursuit through the hollow by a person whose sanity had deserted her.

She should have called Eli, asked him to come to Ben's farm with her. Or let Jerk follow her as he'd been instructed to do. Instead, she'd driven straight into a trap. Yes, she was fit, and she could run. But Orley was hell-bent on killing her, and of the two of them, her cousin knew the hollow best.

Because of that, Sadie had no choice. As much as she hated the thought, she circled back toward the bog, where the ground was slick and balance an ongoing issue. If she could reach the cave she and Eli had used, she might make it back to the road. Road, Bronco, escape.

A sketchy map formed in her mind. So did a picture of Eli's face. But he wasn't here. This was between her and Orley.... And where was the stupid cave entrance?

She wove a haphazard path through the hollow. Were those Orley's footsteps behind her? Was she shouting at her through the fog? Sadie thought she glimpsed a light, but she couldn't be sure and didn't dare slow down to look.

The ground beneath her oozed and almost sent her sliding into the weeds. Determined not to die, she hung on and kept going.

Unlike the shouts, there was no mistaking the thwack of three bullets as they struck a tree directly ahead of her.

Orley would want her to stay visible. Fine. As long as she avoided any direct moonbeams, she'd still present a difficult target.

She hoped.

Sadie's heart hammered louder in her chest. Two more bullets zinged past. Did they come from the same direction as before? Her instincts said no. She had a split second to glimpse the movement, but no time to react as Orley flew out of the darkness and tackled her to the ground.

"Black belt," her cousin grunted, and attempted to work Sadie onto her stomach.

"D.C.," Sadie panted back, and swung the flashlight she still held hard into Orley's ear.

Orley howled and grabbed a handful of Sadie's hair. Ignoring the pain in her skull, Sadie took aim at her cousin's face, then used her fingernails to rake her cheek. When Orley jerked upright, she punched her in the throat and kicked free.

Unfortunately, by the time she scrambled to her feet, Orley was on her knees with the .45 aimed at her head.

"You, Cousin Sadie, are so dead."

A single shot rang out. Freezing, Sadie squeezed her eyes shut and waited for the rush of blackness. To her astonishment, it didn't come. Although her pounding heart drowned out almost every other sound, she thought she heard someone calling her name.

Inching her eyes open, she spotted Orley on the ground. Her left arm was outstretched, and she lay facedown in the mud.

Then suddenly, Eli was spinning her into his arms. Before Sadie could utter a sound, he crushed his mouth to hers and for a blissful moment made all her fears disappear.

If the kiss had never ended, she might have been able to erase everything that had come before. Unfortunately, as she'd told Orley, nothing lasted forever. When Eli raised his head to search her face, the horror flooded back in.

She breathed out slowly. "I don't want her to be dead."

"I know. I'm sorry, sweetheart, I have to…" Framing her face with his fingers, Eli kissed her again, long and deep. "You don't have to look."

"Yes, I do."

He wasn't rough, but Sadie suspected he wanted to be. He knew, and so did she, that Orley would have shot her in a heartbeat if Eli's bullet hadn't struck first.

The groan that emerged from her cousin's throat told Sadie she was alive. The blood on her jacket suggested she might not remain that way for long. With her emotions reeling, Sadie walked around to kneel beside her.

"I aimed for her left shoulder," Eli said. "If she's tough, she'll make it."

Sadie thought of Orley's confession and worked up a

faint smile. "Trust me, Lieutenant, she's tough. She's also determined." As her eyes came to rest on her cousin's face, she sighed. "And very, very sick."

Chapter Twenty-Two

Being a journalist, Sadie knew she'd put all the bits and pieces in order at some point—but she doubted it would happen any time soon.

Ty showed up within ten minutes. Using his two-way, he relayed a message through Ben Leamer's hired hand to the Raven's Cove paramedics. It took a great deal of time and effort, but eventually, Brady and Orley were admitted to the Raven's Cove Hospital and placed under county guard.

By midnight, everyone at Two Toes Joe's Bar had heard some version of the story. By morning, Sadie figured, very little of the factual account would remain. How could it in an area so steeped in lore and legend?

As the tale began to build, Rooney plunked himself between her and Eli and looked grimly from one to the other. "If I'm kin to a murderer, I need to hear the details."

Sadie shook her heard. "You're a Blume, Rooney. Orley and I are Bellams. You're not kin to a murderer. I am."

"Think intent," Eli told her. "He's talking about being related to Brady. It's a fine line between actual and attempted murder."

She sent him a grudging smile. "You're just trying to make me feel better."

"Is it working?"

"Not really." She made herself go back. "In the bog, Orley

talked about the night Laura died. Apparently, while Laura was braiding my hair—babysitting me—right outside the window, Brady was watching her do it. Talk about creepy."

"It's contemptible," Rooney spat. "My great-grandson was a Peeping Tom in high school."

Sadie patted his arm. "He was a lot of things, Rooney, in school and out, but not a murderer. Not even a wannabe twenty years ago. The night Laura died, he was watching her and drinking the coffee that Orley drugged after she 'accidentally' bumped into him at the café. In went just enough ketamine to put him under. Orley hid, waited through a few sips outside my parents' house, then moved in and guided him to an empty lot. A few more sips, and he was out for the night. Knowing that Laura would head back to the Cove as soon as my parents came home, she went to the road that led out of town and waited again."

Rooney gripped his cane a little tighter. "So it was Orley who got Laura to stop, then made her go into the hollow."

"It wouldn't have been an easy drive," Eli remarked. "But at the point of a gun—Orley's father's gun, we'll assume—the difficult became much more possible."

"That's the backstory, Rooney." As she leaned over to kiss his wrinkled cheek, Sadie whispered, "I'll leave the telling of the present-day version in your capable hands."

"Let's call that our cue to leave." Before his great-grandfather could object, Eli stood and drew Sadie to her feet. "Unless you want to stay and help him rearrange the facts to suit."

To grin and mean it felt wonderful—until she saw Ty swaying in his chair across the room while Molly nudged a boilermaker toward him.

"What the…?"

"Let it go, Sadie." Eli set an arm over her shoulders to keep her moving.

"But Ty doesn't drink. Molly knows he doesn't drink."

"Molly's not Orley, and Ty's a big boy."

"I know, but—"

"With a badge."

Shaking it off, Sadie gave his stomach a poke. "Speaking of, Lieutenant, how is it you managed to find me in the hollow?"

He dropped a hard kiss on her lips. "I knew she had you. I called the *Chronicle* and your assistant told me you'd taken your copy editor's Bronco to Ben Leamer's farm."

"Which explains how you located my vehicle, but not how you found me."

"If I say I used my instincts, are you going to go all Raven's Tale on me and suggest I might have been channeling Hezekiah?"

"I would," she teased, "except that Hezekiah wouldn't be tuned in to me so much as my Bellam blood, which would mean I'd have to have been channeling Nola—and I really don't want to go there."

His lips quirked. "In that case, I used criminal logic. Orley murdered Laura in Raven's Bog and got away with it. It stood to reason she'd use the same location again."

"I was looking for the cave when you showed up and shot her."

"I accessed the hollow through the cave."

"Spooky, isn't it?" She caught the hand that dangled over her shoulder and linked their fingers. "As tragic as all of this is, what say we ditch this town, go back to Bellam Manor and make love until Rooney's birthday?"

For an answer, he motioned her ahead of him through the crowd. Sadie took a last bemused look at Molly and Ty, then gave up and stepped outside.

On the dock, she turned to regard Eli. "Brady said he wasn't the monster right before Orley knocked him out.

I know you sort of talked to him at the hospital. Did he give you any details?"

"He only drank a small amount of the tea she brewed for him tonight. There were traces of the tranq she used on the lid of the teapot, and an album filled with computer-altered photographs on the floor. Brady suspected she'd been doping him, so he let her think he was going to settle in for the night with the tea. As soon as she left, he went across the hall and searched her apartment."

"And, lucky for me, found what he was looking for."

"He claimed he was horrified. But under Orley's eagle eye he'd already consumed enough of the tea that he was also disoriented and starting to slide under."

Letting her head fall back, Sadie breathed in the ocean air. "Instead of submitting, he fought the drug's effect, took the Hollow Road and tried to stop her from killing me." She shuddered. "Before the paramedics arrived, Orley told me she murdered a girl named Lisa Johnson right after Brady's senior year."

"Heard that. Brady took Lisa to our senior prom."

"Worse and worse. Orley also swiped a pair of Brady's shoes and muddied them up the night she shot at us with a crossbow. Her father's weapon again. Brady must have thought he was going crazy—or, well, crazier." Bringing her head up, she met Eli's eyes. "Is that why he tried to kill you in the woods near the manor?"

"In for a penny, in for a pound. I don't imagine he thought he had much to lose at that point."

"So how will Rooney spin it in terms of our conjoined legends? Obviously Brady was Ezekiel, and you were Hezekiah."

"And you were Nola. Not sure how he'll work Orley in. As an even darker version of Ezekiel maybe."

Sadie summoned a half smile. "Orley's not a Blume,

Eli. She's my cousin. I honestly can't believe I'm talking about her like this. My own cousin tried to kill me. Legendwise, she'd have to be Sarah."

"There's a Sarah Bellam?"

"In history, yes. In the family archives, not so much. Sarah was Nola's sister. Pretty sure sanity wasn't her strong suit. Oh, and as long as we're tidying this up, Orley also told me that in the process of searching for various chain saws to use on the fallen pine, Brady snuck into the maze and pinned the envelope I found to Hezekiah's cloak. As soon as he saw me go in, he loaded up the chain saw he'd come to borrow and left. He made the call that scared the living hell out of me while he was driving away. That was the same day Orley stole Ben's gun. As for the spike strip, she made that herself, because, well, hey, who hasn't watched cop shows on TV? We both know the rest of the story. And what we don't know really doesn't matter since we're standing here together—with no idea where our lives are headed, but still—standing."

Catching her arm, Eli swung her around and trapped her between the outer wall of Joe's Bar and his body. "We can work on the where, when and how, Sadie. But the with who's not open for debate."

"No?" Hooking her arms around his neck, she stared into his eyes. "Then I guess it's a good thing I love you, Lieutenant Blume. Be warned, however, I'm still a Bellam female. Very high-risk as relationships go."

"Still a cop on this side, Sadie. That's an even higher risk."

She ran a teasing finger over his cheek. "Leaving us with the rather intriguing where, when and how."

Lowering his head, he covered her mouth briefly with his. "Raven's Cove hasn't had a police chief of its own for quite some time. Could be an interesting change of career."

"Okay…" Sadie drew the word out while she played with the ends of his hair. "In that case, and while we're on the subject of interesting, why don't we see what kind of magic we can conjure between us? Think ravens, Eli, and you and me soaring through an autumn night sky. Picture the fog being sucked down into the hollow where it belongs. Then imagine us above it all at Bellam Manor, making love under a gorgeous harvest moon."

He grinned. "I don't have to imagine, Sadie. We're halfway there, and I haven't even formed a thought yet."

"Which in noncryptic language means?"

Only his eyes moved, first to the soft orange moon overhead, then toward the Hollow Road, currently shrouded in layers of filmy white.

"What do you know?" Sadie laughed. "You said I had a knack for predicting the weather. Guess you were right." Smiling, she reached for his mouth. "Might want to brace yourself, Lieutenant." She gave his bottom lip a bite. "The mood I'm in, you never know what else I might have a knack for."

* * * * *

THE SECRET OF CHEROKEE COVE
by Paula Graves

Dana Massey's life is turned upside down, by both a family secret and the offer of protection by the very sexy detective Walter Nix.

"What do you know about the Cumberlands?"

His back stiffened for a second at the sound of the name, and he shot Dana a quick look.

"Why do you ask?" he said.

"My mother's maiden name was Tallie Cumberland. Ever heard of her?"

Dread ran through him like ice in his blood, freezing him as if he was still that little boy from Cherokee Cove who believed every tale his mama told him, especially the scary ones.

"You *have* heard of her."

"I've heard of the Cumberlands."

"Doyle says the most anyone would tell him is that the Cumberlands are nothing but trouble."

"Does that sound anything like your mother?" he asked carefully.

"No."

"Then I wouldn't worry about it."

Dana didn't say anything else until they reached the Bitterwood city limits. Even then, she merely said she'd told Doyle she was going to stay at his house.

"Are you sure you feel safe there?"

"I'm armed, and I'm too wired to sleep."

"I could stick around."

"And protect the poor, defenseless girl?"

"Not what I said."

"I'm usually not this prickly. It's been an unsettling night."

"I'm serious about sticking around. Couldn't hurt to have an extra set of ears to listen out for danger."

"And it wouldn't hurt to have some extra firepower," she admitted. "But it's a lot to ask."

"You didn't ask. I offered."

"So you did." Her lips curved in a smile that softened her features, making her look far more approachable than she had for most of the drive.

Far more dangerous, too, he reminded himself.

"I do appreciate the offer to stay, but—"

"But you're a deputy U.S. marshal with a big gun?"

She patted her purse. "Glock 226."

"Nice." He bent a little closer to her, lowering his voice. "I have a sweet Colt 1991 .45 caliber with a rosewood stock, and if you quit trying to get rid of me, I might let you hold it."

A dangerous look glittered in her eyes. "You're trying to tempt me with an offer to handle your weapon?"

He nearly swallowed his tongue.

She smiled the smile of a woman who knew she'd scored a direct hit. "You can stay," she said almost regally. "We'll negotiate weapon-handling terms later."

*Will Nix's protection be enough to keep Dana safe?
Find out in award-winning author Paula Graves's
THE SECRET OF CHEROKEE COVE,
on sale March 2014 wherever
Harlequin® Intrigue® books are sold!*